THE EXQUISITE CORPSE ADVENTURE

A PROGRESSIVE STORY GAME PLAYED BY

M. T. ANDERSON	GREGORY MAGUIRE
NATALIE BABBITT	MEGAN MCDONALD
CALEF BROWN	FREDRICK L. MCKISSACK
SUSAN COOPER	PATRICIA C. MCKISSACK
KATE DICAMILLO	LINDA SUE PARK
TIMOTHY BASIL ERING	KATHERINE PATERSON
JACK GANTOS	JAMES RANSOME
NIKKI GRIMES	JON SCIESZKA
SHANNON HALE	LEMONY SNICKET
STEVEN KELLOGG	CHRIS VAN DUSEN

CANDLEWICK PRESS

Copyright © 2011 by the National Children's Book and Literacy Alliance

Copyright acknowledgments appear on page 275.

First edition 2011

Library of Congress Cataloging-in-Publication Data
The Exquisite Corpse Adventure / The National Children's Book and Literacy Alliance. — 1st ed.
p. cm.
"An episodic story originally published online by the Library of Congress."
Summary: Twins Joe and Nancy were raised in a circus but on their eleventh birthday they learn their parents are still alive and need their help, so they set out on an adventure filled with many extraordinary beings and adventures. Consists of twenty-seven episodes by nineteen authors and pictures by five illustrators.

[1. Adventure and adventurers — Fiction. 2. Brothers and sisters — Fiction. 3. Twins — Fiction. 4. Animals — Fiction. 5. Robots — Fiction. 6. Space and time — Fiction. 7. Extraterrestrial beings — Fiction. 8. Circus — Fiction.]
I. National Children's Book and Literacy Alliance.
PZ7.E967 2011
[Fic] — dc22   2010040152

ISBN 978-0-7636-5149-7 (hardcover)
ISBN 978-0-7636-5773-4 (paperback)

11 12 13 14 15 16 RRC 10 9 8 7 6 5 4 3 2 1

Printed in Crawfordsville, IN, U.S.A.

This book was typeset in Jenson.

Candlewick Press
99 Dover Street
Somerville, Massachusetts 02144

visit us at www.candlewick.com

CONTENTS

INTRODUCTION

For well over a decade, the National Children's Book and Literacy Alliance (NCBLA) and the Center for the Book in the Library of Congress have worked together in an innovative partnership, promoting and initiating projects and events that energize and excite young people about reading and writing. Dr. John Cole, the founding director of the Center for the Book, has been an honored adviser to the NCBLA since its inception. When Dr. Cole invited the NCBLA to help create a national literacy project for young people as part of its new READ.gov website launch, the NCBLA leaped at the opportunity. *The Exquisite Corpse Adventure* is the lively result of this highly effective and unique partnership.

Originally published on the READ.gov Library of Congress website, *The Exquisite Corpse Adventure* is a buoyant, spontaneous experiment; a progressive story game just like the one many families play on road trips or at home when there is a power outage, and kids play at camps and parties. It is a game in which one person begins a story, stops at a cliff-hanging moment, and the next person picks it up and continues until everyone in the group has the opportunity to contribute. In *The Exquisite Corpse Adventure*, characters spontaneously erupt out of their creators' imaginations; plot lines tumble forth, some realized, some lost; and our plucky protagonists are often left dangling in a moment of peril with their fate unresolved and no logical solution in sight.

Surrealist writer André Breton invented a new twist on the game; that twist inspired our title. At one surrealist social gathering, a piece of paper with the written line *"Le cadavre exquis boira le vin nouveau,"* or "The exquisite corpse will drink the new wine," was passed around the group. Each person added a line, folded the paper to conceal the new addition, and passed it on to the next player. The game became so popular that a visual version was soon added, with players drawing individual parts of the "exquisite corpse."

The contributing writers of *The Exquisite Corpse Adventure* had the opportunity to read all the previous episodes before writing their own individual episode. But the illustrators chose to adhere to the original Exquisite Corpse game premise and did not look at their fellow illustrators' previous contributions before creating art for each new episode.

The contributors to *The Exquisite Corpse Adventure* are some of the most gifted artists and storytellers in our nation. This amazing team of writers and illustrators has made an extraordinary gift, donating their time and talent to a year-long project with the Library of Congress and to the publication of this book. They are so generous and committed because they know that reading can be just as much fun as playing baseball, going to the movies, watching TV. They know that riveting stories offer a healthy escape through which kids can get lost in whole new worlds. They join the NCBLA in believing that all young people must have equal access to exciting and interesting books and information sources that invite them to dream and give them the tools to achieve their dreams.

MARY BRIGID BARRETT
President, Founder, and Executive Director
The National Children's Book and Literacy Alliance

THE EXQUISITE CORPSE

✦ ✦ ✦ ✦ ✦ ✦ ✦ ✦ ✦ ✦ ✦ ✦ ✦ ✦ ✦ ✦

A Very Unusual and Completely Amazing Story
Pieced Together Out of So Many Parts
That It Is Not Possible
to Describe Them All Here, So Go Ahead
and Just Start Reading

✦ ✦ ✦ ✦ ✦

JON SCIESZKA

illustrated by CHRIS VAN DUSEN

This story starts with a train rushing through the night.

The full moon lights the silver rails winding around dark mountains, through deep woods, and over steep gorges of jagged rock and one freezing-cold rushing black mountain river.

I wish there was enough time to describe all of the funny (and touching) twists and turns — especially the Elephant Clown Party — that led up to now. But there isn't. Enough time. Because there is a ticking clock. And the two passengers we care most about don't know anything about it.

In a sleeping berth, in the third car from the end of the train, are two children, eleven-year-old twins, who have just run away from the circus.

The girl's name is Nancy. The boy's name is Joe.

They have no idea that those are not their true names. Though they will figure it out soon enough.

Up until two hours ago, Nancy and Joe thought they were orphans. That turned out to be not true, either.

Joe holds up the birthday card that has suddenly changed their lives.

"This isn't even in code! If our real mom and dad are such secret spies, wouldn't they have at least written in code?"

"Maybe they didn't have enough time," says Nancy.

Happy

HELP. NOW.

FOLLOW CLUES.

RESCUE US BY

PIECING TOGETHER THE EXQUISITE CORPSE.

Birthday.

LOVE, MOM & DAD

"Gets right to the point. And there is this mark. The same mark we both have on our right little toe. Who else would know about that?"

Joe frowns. "But we don't really know if we are going to the right place. We don't really know if the Exquisite Corpse is the Top-Secret Robot we're supposed to piece together. And we don't really know how to help."

Joe is right to be worried. But he is worried for all of the wrong reasons.

The note *is* from their real mom and dad. They *are* going to the right place. The Exquisite Corpse *is* a very Top-Secret

Robot that can only be assembled by them. And because they were raised in a circus, Joe and Nancy have been perfectly trained for just this moment.

Fire juggling, trapeze flips, sharpshooting, bullwhip stunts, lock picking, lion taming, bareback riding, knife throwing, snake charming, disappearing, sword swallowing, and other circus skills can come in handy in all sorts of situations.

What Joe *should* be worried about is the clock — the ticking clock. Oh, so much more to explain. So little time.

Here, you will just have to piece things together yourself:

If the train makes it over the last treacherous gorge, there is a good chance that you and Nancy and Joe will have to deal with werewolves and mad scientists, real ninjas and fake vampires, one roller-skating baby, a talking pig, creatures from another planet (possibly another dimension), killer poetry, clues from classic children's books, two easy riddles, several bad knock-knock jokes, plenty of explosions, a monkey disguised as a pirate, two meatballs, a blue plastic *Star Wars* lunch box (missing its matching thermos), a ticking clock, and not just one bad guy but a whole army of villains, cads, scalawags, sneaks, rats, varmints, and swindlers. Also several desperados, a gang of evildoers, and one just plain bad egg.

And you-know-who will have to piece together the Exquisite Corpse.

But first, the ticking clock.

It is attached to the last bridge.

And, of course, there is a wire that leads from the clock to an entire bundle of dynamite.

Joe and Nancy's train rushes toward that bridge.

The second hand of the clock has exactly forty-seven more ticks before it reaches its very explosive alarm time.

Joe looks once more at their birthday card.

"So now what do we do?"

THE LOST CLUE

✦ ✦ ✦ ✦

KATHERINE PATERSON

illustrated by JAMES RANSOME

Do?" said an ominous yet familiar voice outside their berth. "There is nothing you can *do,* kiddos. In exactly forty-seven ticks of the clock, this train will come to the final bridge, and I do mean *final!*"

"Boppo?" Joe stuck his head out between the curtains to see the painted face and bright red nose he thought they'd left far behind. "What are you doing on this train?"

Boppo laughed. It was an evil unclown-like sound that sent shivers down our heroes' spinal columns. "Did you think you could run away so easily? But, no time to chat. I have to de-train before de train de-molishes." And with that Boppo raced away in the direction of the caboose.

"Pull the emergency cord, Nancy!" cried Joe as he leapt from the berth and gave chase.

Nancy yanked the red handle above the berth. Almost immediately the great train shuddered and squawked to a stop. In the distance she could hear it — a gigantic explosion. She pushed her way down the aisle, which was quickly filling with passengers who were furious at being so rudely awakened. She found Joe staring off the back of the train. Boppo was long gone.

"Nancy, we've got to get off this train. Now. While it's stopped."

"And not warn the police about Boppo?" Nancy was horrified. "No," she said, "first we need to make an anonymous tip. If only we had a cell phone."

"There are lots of people milling around," said Joe. "I'll pickpocket a phone." Joe had picked up a lot of useful tricks working in and around a circus.

"That's dishonest," said Nancy, who was highly moral, "but I guess it's better than letting potential killers get away."

A phone was appropriated from a passenger in the dining car and the authorities were called. With a clear con-

science, our noble twins left the borrowed phone on the rear platform, climbed off the train, and walked forward past the stalled engine. Ahead in the moonlight they could see on their left the shining rails upon a second railway trestle and on the right the twisted metal remains of the bridge their train had been scheduled to cross.

"Now what?" said Joe, peering down into the deep gorge that lay beneath the once-twin spans. "It would take us hours in broad daylight to hike down and up this chasm, and we'd never be able to swim that roaring river at the bottom anyway."

"Fortunately, the moon is bright," said the valiant girl, "and having been raised in a circus, we are expert tightrope walkers. We will walk across the surviving bridge."

"Without a net?"

"Naturally," said Nancy. "Take off your shoes. We'll do it sock-footed."

We won't say that Joe was afraid, but he was a better pickpocket than acrobat. Still, by humming a cheery tune and never, ever once looking down through the gaps between the ties into the abyss or to the side at the mangled wreckage of the destroyed bridge, he managed to follow his sister across the treacherous rail.

"Well," said Joe, "that wasn't so bad. Now all we have to do is follow the clues, find the pieces, put together the Exquisite Corpse, and rescue our parents."

"Look at the birthday card again," said Nancy. "See if it gives us any clue to begin with."

"I left it on the train!" cried Joe. "I've lost our only clue!"

"Perhaps I can help, dearies." Coming toward them out of the night shadows was a sight so frightening, it was almost enough to make them turn and race back across the ominous gorge.

THE FOUND CLUE

✦ ✦ ✦ ✦

KATE DiCAMILLO
illustrated by CALEF BROWN

It was Boppo, of course. His hair was standing up on top of his head in a way that was not at all attractive. It made him look quite mad.

"You should do something about your hair," said Nancy. "It makes you look crazy."

"I am crazy!" shouted Boppo. "Plus, I just walked sock-footed over an ominous gorge. It's enough to make anyone's hair stand on end."

"I can't believe you followed us," said Nancy. "The stealth! The daring!"

"Yes, well," said Boppo, "I have some advice for you: never underestimate a clown."

"What's that noise?" said Joe.

"Do you mean that tick-tick-ticking?" said Boppo.

"Yes," said Joe.

"I hear it, too," said Nancy.

"I thought you kids might like a little show," said Boppo.

"No, thank you," said Nancy. "It's dark. And we're in a hurry."

"Oh, everyone has time to be entertained," said Boppo. He laughed and put a hand in one of his pockets.

"You're not going to juggle, are you?" said Joe.

"Please don't juggle," said Nancy. (Nancy, you will remember, is highly moral; and highly moral people find juggling objectionable.)

"You don't have time to juggle," said Joe. "We called the authorities. They're on their way. You're in big trouble, Boppo."

"Oh, I think not," said Boppo. "Watch very carefully now, dearies. Don't take your eyes off your friend Boppo." Boppo pulled a meatball from his pocket.

"Oh, I hate it when you juggle meatballs," said Joe. "It's so boring."

"And messy," said Nancy.

Boppo pulled another meatball from his pocket. "Shhhh," he said. "Keep your eyes on the clown." He reached into his pocket a third time and pulled out a ticking, humming thing.

"It's a bomb!" said Nancy.

"I guess you can't say juggling is boring now," said Boppo, "can you?" The clown began to juggle the two meatballs and the bomb.

"Oh, Joe," said Nancy, "what should we do?"

"Let's be patient," said Joe.

"Patient?" said Nancy. "Patient! What if while we're being patient, the bomb goes off?"

"Shhhh," said Joe. "It will happen. You know it will. It always does."

"But it's a bomb!" said Nancy.

"Just be ready to use your catlike reflexes," said Joe.

Boppo juggled. Boppo laughed. The meatballs and the bomb flew through the air, faster and faster: meatball, meatball, bomb; meatball, meatball, bomb. The twins braced themselves. And then it happened, just as it always did.

Boppo fell asleep. Mid-juggle. He simply dropped to the ground in a deep and profound and peaceful slumber. A meatball fell on top of him and then another. But before the bomb could hit the ground (or the clown), Nancy (oh, brave, moral Nancy!) made use of her catlike reflexes and reached out and grabbed hold of it.

"Good job, Nancy," said Joe. "Toss it here."

Nancy threw Joe the bomb. Joe turned and threw it off into the darkness. "Teamwork!" said Joe. There was a thump. A wham. And then there was total silence.

Boppo whimpered and then began to snore.

"Narcoleptic clowns are a really sad phenomenon," said Joe.

He bent over Boppo.

"What are you doing?" said Nancy.

"I'm searching his pockets," said Joe.

"Oh, but Joe, that's not moral."

Joe pulled several red noses out of the clown's pocket. The noses were followed by a rubber rat. The rubber rat was followed by a book of poems by Edna St. Vincent Millay. "Clown pockets kind of give me the creeps," said Joe. And then he said, "Wait a minute. Here it is! Our clue, Nancy. Here's our destiny. The card." He stood. He held it over his head.

"Lovely," said a voice, "just exactly super-de-dooper. I'll be taking that, then. Such helpful children."

Dig That Pig

♦ ♦ ♦ ♦

Susan Cooper

illustrated by Timothy Basil Ering

It was a pig. A very large, lean, elegant black pig with a white patch around one eye. He looked exceedingly dangerous. "I'll take it *now*," he said, and he held out his front hoof.

Down on his right hind hoof there was a small red arrow, just like the birthmark the twins had on their right little toes, but they didn't notice that. After all, they were facing a large, threatening pig. And it was dark.

Joe still had Boppo's rubber rat in his hand. Quick as a wink, he thrust it at the outstretched hoof, called telepathically to his twin, and bravely dived off the bridge into the gorge. Nancy dived after him, even more bravely. (Don't you agree? I mean, she'd had an extra moment to think about it.) The river was a long way down, but they had both been making excellent swallow dives from the high trapeze since they were five years old.

Fortunately, the freezing water had been made pleasantly warm by the explosion of Boppo's bomb. The twins had a short but refreshing swim. They clambered ashore, and as they shook themselves dry, they heard a loud splash in the river behind them. Then another. What was happening, out there in the dark water?

"Run!" said Joe.

They ran through the trees, with vampire bats swooping frustrated above their heads, and soon came to a clearing. Given the circumstances, you might expect them to have come upon a gingerbread house and a witch. Instead, they saw in the moonlit clearing a full-size boxing ring, in which an athletic-looking baby was twirling in rapid circles. He wore tiny roller skates, a diaper, and a baseball cap with MAX written on it, and he was laughing.

Outside the ring, a small man was jumping up and down, cracking a bullwhip. They could tell from his shock of

mad white hair that he was Albert Einstein. Or maybe not.
But he was certainly mad.

"Faster! Faster!" shouted Albert Einstein.

"Leave that baby alone!" Nancy called, full of moral fervor. Once in a while her moral fervor got the better of her.

She ran up and seized Albert Einstein's bullwhip, cracking it expertly so that its long leather lash snaked around him and pinned his arms to his sides.

The baby went on roller-skating around the boxing ring, laughing merrily.

"No!" shouted Albert Einstein, struggling to move his pinioned arms. "It's my greatest experiment — we're solving the secret of perpetual motion! E equals MC squared plus . . . something else. We're nearly there!"

Then he stared at Nancy and Joe. "It's you!" he cried. "Artoo and Deetoo! The Corpse twins, on the trail to piece together my Secret Robot! Have you got your passport?"

Joe had the birthday card clenched tightly in one hand; he opened it. "You mean this?" He elbowed his sister. "Nancy — lighten up —"

Reluctantly Nancy gave the bullwhip a twitch, so that Albert Einstein spun like a top and was free.

The baby was roller-skating faster and faster now, singing — quite creditably — the theme from *Star Wars*.

Albert Einstein beamed as he saw the card. "There it is — just in time! You are a credit to your parents, my dears. Max is your clue to the next step on your trail, and you must get there before the sun rises! It's that way!"

He pointed beyond the boxing ring, into the shadows.

But there was a clopping and a rustling sound behind them, and into the clearing came Boppo, riding on the pig.

THE EXQUISITE CORPSE

✦ ✦ ✦ ✦

GREGORY MAGUIRE

illustrated by CHRIS VAN DUSEN

Hold everything," said Boppo.

Everyone obeyed as much as possible. Joe held the birthday card with their parents' urgent cry for help. Nancy held the bullwhip in readiness. The baby held the last note in the *Star Wars* theme song. Einstein held his breath.

"I'm not holding a thing, including you! Get off my back!" snarled the dripping black pig with the white eye patch. Boppo hung on as the pig began to buck like a bronco. "I tell you I'm not joining forces with you!"

"We can work together as villains!" cried Boppo, mopping his clown face with a trail of nine linked handkerchiefs in different colors. "Trust me."

"I *never* trust another villain!" answered the pig. He snorted and contorted so quickly that the eye patch flung off. Without that clever disguise, Joe and Nancy suddenly recognized him as Genius Kelly, the dancing pig from the circus they had tried to run away from but that, increasingly, seemed to be hunting them down.

"Can we stop holding our breath now?" wheezed Einstein.

"You don't need permission to breathe," snapped Nancy. She turned the bullwhip on Boppo the clown and Genius Kelly the dancing pig and bound them together. She snared the pig's hooves in a secondary loop, of which she was particularly proud because it brought the pig into a snout dive right before them all.

Joe, Nancy, the baby, and Einstein stared fiercely at the immobilized pair of evil circus agents.

"I want some answers and I want them now," said Nancy. Her prowess at the bullwhip was going to her head. "First things first. Genius Kelly, I never knew you could talk."

"The world is full of surprises," replied the pig. "Did you know that as Winston Churchill led Britain to victory in World War II, every night he smoked a pink cigar while sitting in a bathtub filled with rubber cement?"

"Is that true?" asked Joe, who, being ninety seconds younger than Nancy, was sometimes gullible.

"All of it. Except the part about Winston Churchill. Never be surprised by surprises; it's bad for the digestion. Did you know that your stage name, Sloppy Joe, is really a cunning code name devised to throw alien enemies off the trail in case they tracked you down to the Sick and Tired Circus?"

"No! I thought it was my stage name because my thinking is sloppy. What with my being so much younger and more immature than Nancy. And constantly reminded about it by Ringmaster, who never let me talk in public. What's my real true name when I am not disguised as Sloppy Joe?"

"Joe Sloppy."

"Clever! No one would ever guess." Joe trusted everyone so nicely. This is a charming trait, if sometimes dangerous.

Nancy asked, "If my stage name is Dancy Nancy, then what's my real name? Nancy Dancy?"

"No," said the pig. "You're his sister. Your real name is Nancy Sloppy."

"I don't think I like that."

"We haven't time to convene a meeting of the Everyone-Feel-Sorry-for-Nancy Club. Your brother has another question. Yes, Sloppy Joe?"

Nancy stuck out her tongue at the pig. Joe said, "Since you're answering questions, what is an Exquisite Corpse?"

"It's a yoga position invented by Winston Churchill at the height of World War II in which you balance yourself on your eyelashes and touch your knees to your adenoids."

"Is that true?"

"All of it. Except the part about Winston Churchill. Actually the position was invented by his evil twin brother, Princeton Churchill."

"Don't listen to a word of this!" shouted Boppo. "Almost every word he says is a lie, including *low-cal* and *de-caf*!"

Nancy drew herself up straight. "Now look. I'm a girl proud of a certain inner compass that guides her right in terms of her —" She paused.

"Morals?" interrupted Boppo and Genius Kelly witheringly.

"Timing," she declared. "It is time for some true answers. I get the feeling Genius Kelly is using his garbled history to distract us from something important. I want to know what an Exquisite Corpse really is before we go any further." Suddenly she gota circus-y sort of idea about how to deal with these lunatics. Clown with them. "Knock, knock," she said.

"Who's there?" they all answered, except the baby.

"Thermos."

"Thermos who?"

"Thermos be an explanation of the Exquisite Corpse, and I want it now."

"That's easy," said Einstein, who out of anxiety, probably, had been trying to crochet his hair into a pot holder. "Listen carefully. You understand that corpses of any sort follow a routine pattern of corruption and decomposition. But if you can manage to get some flitch or bit of a corpse — a fingernail, a dying leaf off a tree, a bird's feather — up to warp speed, you can generate a shadow-thing, an exquisite replica, which might last long enough to be useful. Myself, I experimented with a lock of my baby hair that Mama had saved in a volume of poetry by Edna St. Vincent Millay, and look

what I have now." He indicated his nimbus of white hair. "The grafting was painful but it proves my point. I call the process Renaissance."

"Excuse my sloppy thinking, but I thought the corpse was a robot," said Joe.

"Even a robot can be regenerated by my warp-speed process," said Einstein, "if you start with a useful cog or the right computer chip or maybe a pair of triple-A batteries. And if we get the corpse of a slain robot to regenerate, it might be capable of bringing Nancy and Joe to rescue their mom." He shrugged at the clown-and-pig roll-up as if to say, *Sorry, villains.*

"Didn't we need to rescue both our parents? And didn't you call us Artoo and Detoo?" said Nancy.

"I was just trying to get the baby in the *Star Wars* mood," said Einstein. "I suppose you've guessed there are sometimes glitches in trying to generate an Exquisite Corpse, and the baby is one of them. I hadn't expected to make the introductions just yet, but I suppose, as Genius Kelly advises, never be surprised by surprises. Children, allow me to present your illustrious father, Professor Alistair Sloppy."

"Daddy?" whispered Joe and Nancy.

The baby smiled broadly and wet his diaper, which was, when you come to think of it, not much of a surprise.

SURPRISE! SURPRISE! SURPRISE!

✦ ✦ ✦ ✦ ✦

PATRICIA C. AND FREDRICK L. McKISSACK

illustrated by JAMES RANSOME

No way! I don't believe you!" Nancy said, shaking her head in disbelief. "How can a baby be our father?"

"In one way, he is," said Einstein, quickly adding, "but in two ways, he's not."

"I usually leave solving riddles and other word games to Nancy," said Joe.

"This one's got me stumped," said Nancy.

Einstein shrugged. "It will come to you," he said. Then he pulled a diaper out of his backpack and began drying Max. The baby cooed his gratitude.

Einstein took off the baby's tiny roller skates in order to put on little hiking boots. "You're going to need these, Max," said Einstein.

Could this really be their father? Nancy and Joe moved in closer to see if Max had a red arrow on his little toe. He did.

"Those red arrows are multiplying. They must be clues of some kind," said Nancy.

Joe agreed. Nancy was usually right about such things. "We've got arrows on our toes. Baby Max has one, and . . ."

"So do I!" snorted Genius Kelly, the pig! He had chewed through the whip Nancy had used to bind Boppo the clown to him. The pig was free now and crouched as if to attack anything or anybody who got in his way. "I want that baby!"

Showing more bravery (and maturity) than he'd ever shown in his whole life, Joe stepped in between Max and Genius Kelly. "If — if — if you think I'm going to let you harm this little one," Joe sputtered, or maybe it was more like a mutter, "it aine gonna happen." Nancy cringed when her brother used *aine gonna*. (As you know, highly moral people insist upon good grammar.) Nonetheless, she was still proud of his stand against the dangerous Genius Kelly.

But the pig was totally unimpressed. He charged into

Joe, yelling, "Out of my way!" Joe fell backward into Einstein and both of them went careening over the boxing ring ropes. Now Genius Kelly had a clear path to the baby, who was sitting defenseless on the floor of the ring, clutching his blue plastic *Star Wars* lunch box. Max thought it was all really quite funny and clapped his pudgy little hands and squealed.

As Genius Kelly built up speed, heading for Max, Nancy stuck out her foot and tripped the pig, who slipped, slid, and fell flat on his nose. That gave Joe, who had recovered from his spill, just enough time to snatch the baby from under the ring's bottom rope and run into the woods. Genius Kelly followed, snorting and sniffing and hurling insults and threats like lightning bolts.

Meanwhile, Boppo had freed himself from the whip as well and grabbed an unsuspecting Nancy from behind. "Surprise!" the clown said menacingly. "Okay, Einstein, these woods are infested with all kinds of bad guys, and the leader of them is Leonardo Dubenski."

"He's the worst of the worst," said Einstein.

"But you know these woods like your backyard. I've got to capture that baby and get through those woods before Leonardo Dubenski finds out what's really going on. . . ."

Boppo stopped and his red mouth stretched into a huge, deceptive grin. "See why you've got to help me track that dear little baby?"

"How disingenuous," said Nancy. "And who is this Leonardo person, anyway?"

Boppo scowled. "You'd better hope we don't run into him in the woods. Hey," Boppo added, "let's take the girl along and hide behind her when the villains attack!"

Before Einstein could answer, Boppo's head bobbed forward and instantly he was fast asleep. What a surprise. Or was it?

Nancy pushed Boppo off and he collapsed like a heap of rags. She rushed toward the woods to save her brother and Max, who were no match for an irate pig and a villain even the villains feared.

"Wait, let me get my backpack," said Einstein.

"No way. You're not coming along to hide behind me when we get attacked," Nancy said, heading for the woods. "No way!"

"Knock, knock," Einstein said.

Nancy halted, as Einstein knew she would. She loved knock-knocks. "Who's there?" she asked.

"Russian."

"Russian who?"

"Fools Russian where angels fear to tread," he said. "You need me to get through those woods . . . especially if you run into Leonardo Dubenski."

"O-kay! But I want the answer to the riddle about Baby Max and our father," Nancy countered.

"Better still, I'll take you to the answer."

It didn't take long for Einstein and Nancy to catch up with Joe. What? Another surprise! The three of them — yes, Joe, Max, AND their archenemy, Genius Kelly the pig — were sitting high on a boulder overlooking a stream, sharing a tuna-on-whole-wheat sandwich, cookies, and a tropical fruit cup they'd found in Max's blue plastic *Star Wars* lunch box. "Too bad the thermos is missing," said Genius Kelly. "It might have had some soup in it."

That did it for Nancy. "Joe? How could you? You're laughing like you're with an old friend. This is a dangerous place, not a city park."

"I know that!" said Joe. "Wait until you hear what Genius Kelly has to say." Joe beckoned for Nancy to join them.

Nancy turned to say something to Einstein, but he began to fade in and out, flashing a blue light, until he —

poof — vanished. "No!" shouted Nancy, grabbing a handful of thin air. "Now we'll never know what the riddle means."

Genius Kelly flipped over on his back, kicked up his legs, and let out a shrill, high-pitched squeal that sounded like . . . laughter. Laughter? Baby Max did the same thing, except his little squeals weren't nearly as intimidating.

Nancy looked at the pig, Max, and her brother. "What's so funny? Who's gonna help us get through these villain-infested woods now?"

"Nancy, you said *gonna*!" said Joe.

"Not to worry," said the pig. "Einstein was just a hologram I programmed to say things I couldn't say and do things I couldn't do. The riddle is really mine."

"See, Nancy," said Joe. "I told you. . . . Not bad for someone they say is a sloppy thinker."

The pig continued to explain the riddle. "Little Max is your father in *one way*, because he has Professor Alistair Sloppy's DNA. But in *two ways* Max is not your father, because, one, Max is a failed experiment designed to get your father back to this dimension. And two, the real Professor Alistair Sloppy and his wife (your mother), Elizabeth Verrie-Sloppy, are trapped in a time warp, a dimension from which they cannot return."

"Well, for sure, you're no ordinary pig," said Nancy. "Who are you, really?"

"Among my many names, I am known as Axan. I am from that other time dimension. Your parents were worried sick about you being on this side, but they were unable to get home to you. So I made the leap to this side. And I have watched over you all your lives, while your parents worked on a way to make the journey back home," the pig explained. "What better place to hide than the Sick and Tired Circus?"

"Well, actually, really, any place would have been better than the Sick and Tired Circus," said Joe.

"I want to know why you choose to be so mean to us," Nancy said. "We thought you were a villain."

"That's what I wanted others to think. That way, I always knew who was up to no good. Who would ever suspect a pig — a talking pig at that?"

"Tell her what the red arrows mean," Joe said.

But they were interrupted. "Aren't we a cozy little gathering?" said someone on the ledge above them. There was nothing familiar or friendly about the voice.

THE BEAST PIT

✦ ✦ ✦ ✦ ✦

SHANNON HALE

illustrated by CALEF BROWN

Joe, do the Flying Watermelon!" Nancy said.

Without hesitation, Joe performed a backflip off the tree branch. While he was still midair, Nancy tossed Baby Max in a graceful arc (he weighed about the same as the watermelons they used back in the circus). Joe landed on the forest floor, his arms outstretched, and the baby plopped safely in his hands, while Nancy leapt after them hands-first, then finished off with a cartwheel. She bowed automatically before remembering there would be no applause in these villain-infested woods — only certain death.

"Run!" said Joe.

And so they ran — away from the unfamiliar and unfriendly voice that had startled them out of the tree, away from the boxing ring beside the river, away from the stopped train and bridge wreckage — far away from all the strange events that had shaped their life into a nightmare. They ran, but not fast enough. It was one thing to catch a baby/watermelon in a spectacular circus stunt, but another to lug one through the woods. Joe panted with the effort.

And just where was Genius Kelly? Nancy was turning to look when a shadowy figure dropped out of a tree, moonlight glinting on her long knife.

The twins veered away, but another shadowy figure appeared, and another, until Joe, Nancy, and the baby were encircled by dozens of men and women in frighteningly black garb, all with moon-licked daggers, all smiling in a supremely villainous manner. The smiles gave Joe the creeps. Nancy didn't notice the smiles, being suitably creeped out by the daggers. But Baby Max was enchanted by the glinting of moonlight. It made the daggers look wet and sweet.

Baby Max said, "Lollipop."

Joe held the baby tighter. Nancy raised her hands in a karate pose and turned slowly, daring the villains to attack.

"Now, don't be foolish," said the unfamiliar and unfriendly voice behind them.

Into the circle of shadowy figures strode a man so large,
so horrifying, so disquieting, that I tremble to describe him.
Let me simply say that his rear was where his face should be
and his rear . . . spoke.

"I am Leonardo Dubenski, Lord of Thieves, and these
are my loyal followers."

He was dragging poor Genius Kelly by his ears and
dumped him beside the twins.

"We're too late," the pig whispered. "Leonardo Dubenski
found the Exquisite Corpse."

"Bad," said Baby Max, pointing at Leonardo, who had offset his horrific visage by putting on a jaunty hat.

"Indeed," said Nancy. She was getting a bad feeling about all this.

But Joe giggled. Sure, they were facing death by a cowled horde of thieves, but really, can you blame him? The man's bum-head was speaking, and with an Eastern European accent.

Leonardo picked Joe up by his hair, and our valiant boy's laugh squeaked to a stop.

"You find my appearance humorous, boy?" Leonardo boomed. "I assure you, before yesterday, I was quite becoming. Isn't that so, minions?"

The thieves muttered quick assent.

"But last night I discovered something hidden in *my* woods, and when I touched it, the *thing* exploded, turning me into this monstrosity! You trespassers are responsible; I can feel it in my whiskers. Tell me how to undo its dark deeds, or your lives end before dawn!"

"I don't know. . . ." said Joe, trying not to whimper. His hair really hurt.

"Let him go!" said Nancy.

Genius Kelly whimpered. "No way to fix things now. Hopeless. . . ."

Leonardo dropped Joe and roared an angry roar that sounded like he'd eaten some bad meat.

"To the beast pit!" yelled the Lord of Thieves, and his horde of minions cheered.

In moments, Joe, Nancy, Genius Kelly, and Baby Max were tied up together in yards of thick rope and dangling from a hook. Beneath them yawned a pit of disturbing depth, and from its disturbing depths came snaps and growls of such horror, they could only be produced by ferocious beasts. Of the biting variety. Biting and tearing and eating.

"For shame!" Nancy yelled as the villains lowered them into the pit. "Picking on two kids, a baby, and a pig. Haven't you anything more constructive to do with your time?"

The shadowy figures only smiled as they lowered our captive heroes into the subterranean darkness. The growls and hisses grew louder.

Joe said, "I hope it doesn't hurt to die."

Nancy said, "I wish we could have met our parents."

Baby Max said, "Lollipop."

Genius Kelly growl-oinked. "I'm sorry, children. Our

plan failed. I hid the pieces of the Exquisite Corpse in these villain-infested woods, where I thought they would be safe from everyone . . . except —"

"The villains themselves," said Joe.

"Right," the pig said sadly.

Nancy struggled against the ropes, but it was useless. Down they went. Lower, lower . . .

"I thought the broken robot would stay hidden until sunrise," said the pig. "But clearly Leonardo found it. You see, the Exquisite Corpse is extremely powerful, and so came with a protective mechanism. Only someone with Sloppy DNA can handle the pieces without suffering . . . consequences."

Leonardo, watching their descent from above, scratched

his cheek and "burped." Nancy shuddered. Not because of the burp (though that *was* morally objectionable). But just how did Leonardo *see* them?

"Your parents wanted to leave you out of all this," Genius Kelly continued, "and so we constructed Max, a clone of your father. He has Sloppy DNA, you see, and we hoped that with the Einstein hologram's help, he could assemble the robot alone. But his baby hands were too small, and we couldn't risk waiting for him to grow any bigger. So we hid the Exquisite Corpse and I came back for you. I felt sure the three of you together could successfully reanimate the robot and use it to save your parents. But now it's too late."

"It's never too late!" Nancy said pluckily.

"That's right," said Joe, somewhat less pluckily. They were nearing the bottom of the pit, where death by beasts awaited. "As Ringmaster used to say, the show must go on."

"I don't see how," said the depressive swine. "When Leonardo touched the Exquisite Corpse, the protective mechanisms not only . . . *maimed* . . . him but also caused an explosion that launched each of the pieces to unknown locations. It would be impossible to track them all down. Unless . . . unless the red arrows can direct us not to the whole cache but to each individual piece. . . ."

◆ ◆ ◆ ◆ ◆

"So that's what they're for!" Nancy reached through the ropes and tore off her shoe. The little red mark on her pinky toe no longer pointed forward, but due east, where the morning sun was just breathing gold into the black sky.

Joe pulled off his own shoe to see that his arrow mark pointed in the same direction as his sister's. His shoe slipped from his hand into the depths, and the beasts yowled and snorgled and ripped it to bits.

"The arrows will lead us to each piece of the Exquisite Corpse," she said, "and once we have them all —"

"We can rebuild it and go free our parents from that nasty other dimension!" said Joe.

"But in order to succeed, we must stay alive," said the pig.

That prerequisite seemed unlikely. They were so deep in the pit now, Nancy could feel the spray of beast saliva on her bare foot. Joe shed one silent tear.

"Lollipop," said Baby Max again. Only this time, the twins noticed that he was holding something — a silver dagger.

"Well done," Joe said, admiring the work of a fellow pickpocket.

The baby beamed.

"But just this once," said Nancy, who couldn't encourage a baby to play with daggers, even with lives on the line. She pried the weapon from the baby's sticky hand and assessed their situation.

Above them, at the edge of the pit, Leonardo Dubenski and dozens of weaponed thieves watched their descent. Below them, the darkness crawled with noxious beasts. They had one dagger between them. And in precisely three seconds, a creature with blood-stained teeth would leap for Joe's throat.

A POSSIBLE SOLUTION

✦ ✦ ✦ ✦ ✦

NATALIE BABBITT

illustrated by TIMOTHY BASIL ERING

One second is not a lot of time, but it was all that was needed. A new voice, the high shriek of a crone, came out of nowhere: "Run! *Run,* you ugly Leonardo Dubenski, with your thieves and beasts! That baby you see there is a wonder baby, and his plan is to turn you all into daffodils!"

Daffodils! To face the wretched weather alone in a weedy field or be crammed rootless into a crowded vase where life is brief—these very thoughts were horrors to Dubenski and his crew. At once there was a scramble for safety: the sound of pounding feet and paws. And then — silence. They were gone.

"Who are you, you with the warning?" cried the pig. "Let us see you!"

And so, from behind a bush, a crooked, bent old woman stepped out. She was wearing a cloak of black, and her hair was frizzy white around her creased and wrinkled face. "I am the voice," she croaked, "but I don't deserve the credit. I am only a reporter of possible things to come. I am Sybil Hunch, the local misfortune-teller. I was reading my crystal ball," she told them, holding out a sphere of misty glass, "and it let me know there was trouble waiting for Dubenski. But it didn't mention *you*. Nevertheless, your danger, like his, is past. I will finish it off with a wave of my hand." And suddenly the rope that had tied them together over the pit became a simple twist of ivy. Nancy, Baby Max, Joe, Genius — all four — swung easily to safer ground and, breaking the vine, dropped to the grass.

"We can't thank you enough, Miss Hunch!" said Nancy, lifting up Baby Max and cuddling him in her arms. "But I didn't know Baby Max was a wonder baby who could change bad people into daffodils."

"I didn't know it, either," replied the crone. "But it seemed like a good idea. There must be something useful for daffodils to do."

"Daffodils, daisies, dandelions, who cares?" cried Joe. "Now we can go on with our project —"

"Our project," Nancy interrupted, "to rescue our mother and father from some other dimension."

"A time warp, is that it?" croaked Sybil Hunch. "I guessed as much. But you've been all through these terrible woods, correct? And found next to nothing of any help at all. I will look into my crystal ball and see if it has anything to say."

They all sat down on the grass there, in a circle, with the crystal ball set in the middle. Sybil Hunch stroked its smooth glass lightly with the tips of her knobby fingers and murmured to it, over and over: "Hmm la hoodle, hmm la hi, doom and gloom, hello, good-bye." The crystal ball began to glow. A cloud moved inside it — faint but growing darker — and its colorless color turned slowly into greens and blues tumbling and rolling over themselves, with rising and falling spreads of lacy white. And as they watched, wide-eyed, a shape appeared, a shape like that of a graceful fish with glittering scales, and a voice came from it, a voice full of bubbles:

"If you've lost your A,
*   And you can't find B,*
Then you have no choice
*   But to go to C."*

And then the sound went silent, the glass's color faded, and it lay inanimate on the grass.

"There is your answer," said Sybil Hunch.

"What answer?" protested Genius Kelly with a snort. "What does it mean, 'go to C'?"

A moment of puzzlement, and then Nancy exclaimed, "Why, it means we should go to *sea*! Salt water! Of course — that's it! We should find the ocean and look for our mom and dad there!"

"But there's no ocean near here," said Joe. "We'd have to travel for days!"

"No, you wouldn't," said Sybil Hunch. "It's only yards away, beyond that hill." And she pointed over Joe's shoulder. "There's a sea right there, the Saline Solution Sea. Perhaps it holds the answers."

Nancy climbed to her feet and tucked Baby Max into the curve of her arm. "There's no time to lose," she said soberly. "Let's go, everyone. Let's go at once."

"You should do exactly that," said Sybil Hunch. "But I will stay behind. My work is here, among these trees, doing what misfortune-tellers do. But I will remember this day forever. I wish you good luck, my dears. May everything go well!"

The crystal ball, however, seemed to expect some other outcome. It rested at her feet, motionless, but if you listened with care, you could hear, coming from its depths, the sound of distant thunder.

IN ARM'S WAY

✦ ✦ ✦ ✦ ✦

NIKKI GRIMES

illustrated by CHRIS VAN DUSEN

Nancy was none too fond of thunder. (It had something to do with her being shot out of a cannon one time too many as a young child.) Fortunately, she had no inkling of the coming storm.

Nancy, Joe, Max, and Genius Kelly pressed on to the hill and the sea beyond. It seemed to Joe that they had been walking for quite some time and still there was no sea in sight.

"I thought Miss Hunch said the sea was a few yards away," said Nancy.

"Maybe she meant that in fortune-teller time," quipped Joe.

"That would be *mis*fortune-teller time," Nancy corrected him.

"Whatever," said Joe. Sometimes his sister could be a pain. But why argue with her? He preferred to save his breath for the journey.

Nancy noticed that the sky had begun to darken. The swirling clouds seemed ominous. Even Max whimpered in the gathering gloom.

"It's okay, Max," said Nancy. "I'm sure we'll get across the sea before the storm hits."

Before long, the scent of the sea tickled their noses, and the party picked up its pace. Except for Genius Kelly, that is. His hoof-steps grew slower with each whiff of salty sea air.

"What's wrong?" asked Nancy.

"Who said anything was wrong?" snorted the pig.

"Well, don't bite my head off," said Nancy.

"We're almost there," said Joe. "Hurry!"

"Wait," said the pig, coming to a full stop. Joe turned and studied him carefully.

"I get it," declared Joe. "You're afraid!"

"No, I'm not."

"Yes, you are."

"No, I'm not!"

"Yes, you are!"

"No, I'm —"

"Stop it!" said Nancy, getting a headache.

"All right!" said Genius Kelly. "I'm afraid of water. Are you happy now?"

"Afraid of water?" said Nancy. "That's silly." At that very moment, a thunderclap reduced her to shivers.

"I suppose everyone is afraid of something," she allowed. "But what are you going to do? You heard Miss Hunch. If we're going to find our parents, we have to cross the sea."

"Swimming's not the only way to cross a sea," said the pig. "I'll just find a place shallow enough to walk across. I'd take you with me, but you're too slow. See you on the other side!" And with that, he took off, calling over his shoulder, "May the force be with you!"

"Pigs," said Nancy. "You just can't trust them."

Her words were drowned out by the next thunderclap. Joe noticed his sister flinch and laid a hand on her shoulder.

"We'll be fine on our own," he said, suddenly the braver of the two. "Come on."

Joe, Nancy, and Max made their way to a clearing that

ended in a cliff edge. Joe peered over the side. There, a mile or so down, was the sandy shore and the sea. Now all they had to do was rappel down the cliff face.

"No one mentioned a cliff," said Nancy.

"Or a gorge," said Joe. "Or a bomb, or a talking pig — or a way down."

"All right!" said Nancy. "You've made your point."

That settled, Joe searched until he found a vine long enough to rappel them to the sand below. He double-looped one end around a sturdy tree root, then handed the other end to Nancy.

"Women and children first," he said, then added quickly, "Just kidding!"

Nancy gave Joe a look that made him wither, then took off her belt and cinched Max tightly to her back. "Hold on tight, Max." He giggled in response, loving the adventure.

Nancy started lowering herself down. At first, Joe could hear her labored breathing and occasional grunts. Then, quite suddenly, the vine went slack and there was only silence.

"Nancy?" called Joe. No response. Joe's heart pounded.

"Nancy!" There was still no answer. Afraid at what he'd find, Joe peered over the cliff's edge.

"Your turn," called Nancy, tossing the vine up toward

her brother. "There's a great footpath here. We can walk down the rest of the way."

Joe wiped the sweat from his brow. "Well, you could have told me!"

Once Nancy's feet hit the sand, she looked around. A small reed basket on the water's edge caught her eye. It was just the right size to hold Max as they journeyed across the sea. By the time she loosened her belt and let Max slide onto the sand, Joe had joined her.

She was just about to lift Max into the basket so they could be on their way when she felt a foreign presence. In one smooth move, she passed the baby to Joe, and took a kung fu stance, ready to kick the daylights out of whatever new villain was stalking them.

"Show yourself!" Nancy demanded.

Out of the darkness of a cave appeared a pirate, skin rich as ebony, robe and bejeweled hands flashing gold. However, Nancy's eagle eyes noticed that his hands were too manicured for a real pirate.

"Who are you?" demanded Nancy.

"That ain't the question, dahlin'. What're y'all doin' out here in the middle of nowhere, all by yourselves, hmm? This ain't no place for kids to be roamin'.'"

Nancy cringed with each *ain't*, dropped *g*, and mangled syllable. She stopped counting the ways in which this person's language was objectionable.

"What's your name?" asked Joe, not wanting to be left out of this interchange. The pirate who wasn't a pirate burst into a blinding smile.

"Ma friends call me Angel. Heck, ma enemies call me Angel, too."

"Angel what?"

"Why, the Angel Who Sat by the Door, of course."

"What door?" Nancy perked up. Could this be another clue?

"Door? Who said anythin' about a door?"

"You did."

"Did I? What're y'all doin' out here, again?" he asked, changing the subject.

"What were *you* doing out here?" asked Joe, feeling especially clever.

"I was out here doin' what I always do. Watchin'."

"Watching what?" Joe was determined to pin him down.

"I already told ya! You young folks just don't listen these days," said Angel.

Nancy sputtered, exasperated. As for Joe, he suddenly

felt like Alice in Wonderland, unable to get straight answers out of anyone after she slid down that rabbit hole. (Okay, so he had swiped Nancy's copy of the book and read it. But who could resist a story about a giant rabbit with a pocket watch?)

"We're wasting time," said Joe. "We need to get going if we're going."

Nancy nodded, got Max settled inside the reed basket, gave him a slight push, and waded into the water after him. She reached for the basket to hold it steady, but just as her fingers grazed the edge, lightning blasted across the sky. In the sea's reflection, Nancy saw a man and a woman, their faces pressed against a door. The image lasted only a brief second, but Nancy's heart told her that these were her parents and that they were calling out to her.

Max cried, and Nancy snapped to.

"Oh! Max!" The basket was drifting out to sea. The peals of thunder were deafening now, but Nancy pushed past her fear and swam as fast as she could. Her short stint as a circus mermaid sure came in handy. She sliced through the water quickly, fighting against the current, heading to the point where the sea began to widen. If she didn't reach him in time . . .

A few more feet, thought Nancy, calling up all her

reserves. *I'm coming, Max!* Nancy grabbed hold of the basket just before the stiff current swept it, and Baby Max, away.

With both in tow, Nancy swam safely to the opposite shore.

Heart beating wildly, Nancy lifted Max from the basket and rested on the bank, cradling him. A few minutes later, Joe clambered up onto the bank himself.

"What took you so long?" she asked, now that she had her breath back.

"Just before I stepped into the water, the pirate tossed a bottle into the sand right in front of me. There was something in it."

"What?"

"This," said Joe, holding up a piece of paper folded around a key.

Guard this key with your life, read the note. *Godspeed, Joe and Nancy. When you see your folks, tell them Angel sends his felicitations.*

Angel had not been there just to annoy them, after all, Nancy realized.

"I don't know what this key opens," said Joe.

"I do," said Nancy, smiling.

"Let's go find our parents."

Nancy held Max up to Joe, and the three were on their way. After taking a few steps, Nancy stubbed her toe on something.

"Ouch!" She bent down to move the object from her path. It was a strange metal alloy, covered with ash from a fire, perhaps, or from an explosion. She was just about to toss it into the brush when sunlight broke through the clouds and she saw the object for what it was. An arm. A robot's arm.

"Well, I'll be," Nancy whispered.

"Joe! Look!"

"My, my," said a raspy voice. "What have you got there?"

WOLF AT THE DOOR

✦ ✦ ✦ ✦ ✦

MEGAN McDONALD

illustrated by JAMES RANSOME

The disembodied voice seemed to come from nowhere and everywhere — ricocheting off rocks, echoing through trees, speaking out of thin air. But try as they might, Nancy and Joe could not lay eyes on the being that belonged to the spooky voice that had just rasped, *What have you got there?*

"Who are you?" Nancy asked, speaking to the air. She trembled; her fingers let go of the robotic arm. It dropped to her feet.

"Show yourself," demanded Joe, trying to muster the same courage he'd shown when he'd thrown himself between Baby Max and Genius Kelly.

"That arranged can be," said the voice in a half-mocking tone. "Riddle me this if you dare to see me in my true form."

It has been said that our intrepid heroes were no strangers to riddles, but this — this lone, throaty voice — seemed to speak in riddles itself.

Joe stood a bit taller. Nancy plucked up her courage. "Wol-wol-wol," babbled the baby.

"Not now, Max," Joe warned. "No lollipops."

"Here, I'll take him for a while," Nancy offered. Joe handed the baby to his sister. She bundled him tighter, holding him close to her pounding chest, heartbeat to heartbeat.

The voice, made only of sound and air, sent goose bumps up and down Nancy's spine. Joe looked around wildly, trying to find a presence.

It was as if the trees themselves were speaking. "Here my riddle then goes:

Thirty white horses upon a red hill
Now they champ, now they tramp, now they stand still."

Silence. The only sound was the toothless bite of the wind rattling the last leaves on the trees. Or was it?

Like a long-ago lullaby once sung to them by their parents, the twins knew the answer. But it was buried deep, in layers of memory now cobwebby with time.

"Thirty white horses? Could it be a snowstorm?" Nancy guessed.

"Upon a red hill. . . . Clouds at sunset?" Joe ventured.

"Piano keys?" Nancy called out urgently.

Joe thought of the merry-go-round that had serenaded them throughout their orphan years. "Carousel?" he uttered desperately.

With each guess, the voice howled with laughter, mocking them.

Just when they felt the gloom of despair in the pits of their empty stomachs, the twins came to the answer, shaking off their slumber at the exact same moment.

"Teeth!" they exclaimed simultaneously, solving the riddle.

As though an incantation had been uttered, the twins heard a deafening sound crack open the earth, deep as the pit of noxious beasts they'd narrowly escaped. Up out of

that crack grew a massive tree trunk, shaggy and gnarled, wreathed in a rope of ivy. The tree bent; four sinewy limbs sprung from its sides. Rough bark turned to coarse hair, yellow eyes blazed, and the great beast before them—all teeth—lunged at them with razor-sharp fangs.

Joe and Nancy were knocked senseless to the ground.

When the earth stopped spinning, Nancy gasped in disbelief at the sight of her own empty arms. Her head still splitting with lightning pain, she came to realize that something, *someone*, had been ripped from her. "Max? Where's Max?" she pleaded.

The monster wolf was gone, but so was the baby!

"Hurry up, Joe!" Nancy urged, still in shock. She struggled to stand, brushing foul-smelling fur from her clothes. "We have to rescue Max!"

But Joe was frantically crawling on hands and knees, desperately searching the underbrush. When he stood, his leaden feet wouldn't lift to follow his sister. "We can't! The key! I had it in my hand. But when I fell back, I saw it fly through the air. The note said to guard it with our lives. We can't just walk away, or we'll never find our parents."

"Then there's only one way," Nancy said in an almost whisper.

"Not that. No. Never," Joe protested. The same blood that ran through Joe's veins also coursed through Nancy's heart. In all their eleven years, they'd never been apart, and Joe was not about to split up now.

"Joe! Look!" Nancy yelped, pointing to the arrow on his right little toe. It pointed south, in the direction of the sea.

"That's it! The key's been cast to the bottom of the sea." But no sooner had he spoken than he peered at the matching red arrow on Nancy's right toe. For the first time in their lives, it pointed in the opposite direction. North. For the first time in their lives, they'd have to go their separate ways. Alone. Lone. Lonely.

The twins had no choice but to utter a good-bye.

With no time to waste, Joe turned in the direction of his arrow, determined to find the key. He headed for the sea, the salt sea, salty as an ocean of tears. He knew better than to look back.

But if he had, he would have seen his sister tear a piece of cloth from the hem of her shirt to stanch the bleeding of a deep scratch caused by the monster wolf as it wrenched

Baby Max from her arms. He would have seen her pick up the robotic arm, her own left arm dangling useless at her side, three perfect drops of crimson blood trailing behind her.

Nancy herself had no inkling how one menacing scratch had changed everything, to the core of her own Sloppy DNA.

A SECOND ARM

◆ ◆ ◆ ◆ ◆

written and illustrated by
STEVEN KELLOGG

Joe had never felt so alone and, indeed, he had never been so alone. He swam steadily out to sea, but inside he was shaken, confused, and distressed knowing that Nancy, his devoted companion, his best friend since birth, and the only family he had ever known, might be in trouble. And he soon might be in trouble as well. And for the first time ever, they wouldn't be able to help each other. That thought threatened to throw him into complete despair, but then his good sense and his natural bravery kicked in. He forced himself to focus clearly on his immediate goal, which was the recovery of the lost key. *Accomplish that,* he told himself firmly, *and then return to shore and search for Nancy.*

Joe filled his lungs with a huge gulp of air and dived straight down. Fortunately, his circus training had a required reading list that included a book by Houdini. It had given Joe some tips on underwater survival, like swallowing and storing several hours' worth of oxygen, as he had just done, and projecting words in air bubbles, which he and Nancy had mastered so that they could talk to each other while they were submerged in the circus penguin pool.

Once he had reached the floor of the sea, Joe spotted an odd serpentine creature emerging from a cave. It snatched a passing fish, deposited it back in the cave, and then reemerged. Joe was about to send the serpent some musical notes encased in bubbles that were part of a snake-charming melody that he and Nancy had practiced on cobras and adders in the circus. But suddenly it became clear that what he had taken for a serpent was actually another robotic arm! Joe waved to see if he could catch its attention. The robotic arm froze in alarm. But after a moment, as Joe continued to smile and wave, it tentatively waved back. Joe slowly approached it with his hand extended in a welcoming gesture. "I hope that we can be friends," he said. "My name is Joe." Very timidly the robotic fingers unclenched and reached toward Joe's hand. The moment their fingers touched, Joe gasped and stared in amazement. The robotic arm had quite magically transformed itself into a real arm!

The new arm reached for Joe, but this time it was not tentative. It grabbed his hand and shook it firmly and vigorously. Then it encircled him in a warm and grateful hug.

"Who are you?" asked Joe. "Where did you come from? How did you get here? Oh, I wish you could talk to me."

In response the fingers of the arm began to move in sequences that Joe recognized as a form of sign language. "Are you trying to say *danger?*" he asked. The arm gave a thumbs-up in affirmation, and then it pointed slowly and ominously toward the cave.

Not wanting to be distracted from his search for the key, or from his plan for a prompt reunion with Nancy, Joe explained the importance and urgency of achieving these goals as quickly as possible.

To his surprise the arm indicated that the key was in the cave. Joe was stunned. He couldn't believe his good luck. "I'll get it right now!" he cried. "And then we can hurry back to rejoin Nancy. That is," he added, "if you would like to come with me. And I hope that you will. You see, my sister has another robotic arm, and . . ."

Joe had been about to explain some of the details of the Exquisite Corpse mystery, but he froze as a grotesque creature slunk out of the cave's shadows.

The beast appeared to be part human and part squid, and it reared up, confronting Joe with eight tentacled arms that writhed and coiled menacingly.

"That arm is my slave!" hissed the squid. "Like you, it trespassed onto my territory! And since it was a pitiful, brainless, robotic fragment with no memory and no future, I placed it under the control of my brain. But now I see that you have had the audacity to release it from its robotic state and to usurp my control. And now *my* slave is loyal to *you*! That is intolerable!"

The squid tried to seize the arm, but it clung desperately to Joe.

"Hold on!" cried Joe. "Let's talk this over! First of all, I haven't come here to trespass or cause trouble. I'm looking for an important lost key, and the arm tells me that I will find it in that cave."

"There it is, and there it shall remain!" snarled the squid. "RELEASE MY SLAVE AT ONCE!"

The arm signaled frantically that it would never submit to enslavement again. It wrapped itself more tightly around Joe, who wanted very much to help it but had no clue as to how he should go about it.

Now . . . we know that the twins had a degree of familiarity with the martial arts, and Joe wondered if the squid might back off if he demonstrated a few karate or kung fu moves. Probably not, Joe decided, as the squid became more threatening, flailing its tentacles and shrieking: "UNHAND THAT ARM! UNHAND THAT ARM! UNHAND THAT ARM!" It seemed dangerously close to exploding into attack mode.

"My sister, Nancy, would say that is a very silly, ill-conceived sentence," said Joe, who was stalling for time while desperately trying to come up with a plan. "She would say that 'Unhand that arm' is as silly as 'Disarm that elbow,'" he continued.

The squid dismissed Joe with a savage hiss and lunged again for the arm. The arm grasped Joe even more firmly and would not be pried loose.

At that moment, thinking of Nancy while the arm gripped him with the strength of a wrestler, Joe thought of a course of action. It would be risky. The physical exertion demanded might exhaust the remainder of his air supply. But it was a plan that called for fairness and sportsmanship, so he was sure that it would meet with Nancy's approval, and there was no doubt that she would applaud his commitment to the arm's freedom. *I only hope I can pull it off,* thought Joe nervously. *Oh, well. . . . Here goes!*

Joe cleared his throat and lowered his voice to an authoritative, take-charge, very grown-up register. "Now, see here, Squid," he began. "If you will calm yourself and think in a rational manner, I'm sure it will be clear to you that these wild threats and outbursts of violence are unmanly and unsquidly. We have an opportunity to settle this dispute in a fair and sportsmanlike manner. In accordance with the laws of knighthood, the code of dueling, and the rules of the Olympic Games, I propose a sporting competition to decide the status of this arm, as well as the ownership of the key. In consideration of the fact that the athletic versatility of my friend has obvious limitations, the only event in which he is fully qualified to compete is classical arm wrestling, and we challenge you here and now to a match."

The squid smirked as it sized up this small, pretentious opponent and his pathetic fragment of a partner. The challenge was accepted.

Joe and the arm exchanged a bravely cheerful thumbs-up and positioned themselves in front of their glowering adversary.

Joe gripped two tentacles in each hand, and the arm encircled the other four. The squid abruptly lunged forward in an attempt to steamroller the teammates off their feet, but they braced themselves and held fast. Then slowly and inexorably, combining every ounce of their strength with their shared determination to win both the arm's freedom and the key, they turned, twisted, and tilted the straining and gasping squid until its balance became precarious. Joe cried, "TWO HEAVE-HOS, AND OVER HE GOES!"

Furious to find itself on the verge of defeat, the squid violently shoved back, hissing like a steam engine. But that shove had no impact. The arm seemed to be gaining power, while the intense exertion of the struggle had clearly depleted the squid's energy. Unfortunately Joe's air reserves had also been depleted, and he knew that within a few minutes he would have to bolt for the surface. Joe decided to pull back and conserve his last precious breaths, while, at the same time, allowing the arm to single-handedly achieve the victory over his former oppressor. The arm seemed to read Joe's thoughts, for, suddenly, with an amazing surge of strength, and seemingly without effort, he lifted the squid high off the sea floor and then flipped it onto its back, decisively winning both the match and his freedom.

The arm pumped ecstatically and high-fived and hugged Joe. When their offer of a sportsmanlike handshake was rejected by the sulking squid, they bid it a hasty farewell, grabbed the key, and swam to the surface. Joe saved his last puff of stored oxygen to exhale with an explosive cheer as he and the arm burst into the open air like a pair of joyful porpoises.

As they swam together and chatted contentedly, Joe was pleased to realize how completely he had learned to understand the arm's sign language. He also realized with a certain sense of surprise how warmly he felt toward the arm. He was such an admirable, kind, and generous arm, as well as a mysterious one. Joe looked forward to getting him together with Nancy and the robotic arm so they could try to figure out how they all related to the Exquisite Corpse puzzle. Meanwhile the arm propelled them through the waves with powerful, sweeping strokes, returning them to shore in a much shorter time than Joe had taken on the way out. It made Joe smile to see how much the arm was enjoying his freedom. *And I am certainly feeling very much better,* he reflected. *I have brought back both the key and a new friend — but now I must find Nancy! I must!*

Once on the beach, the friends collapsed to rest and to dry off in the sun. The arm wistfully told Joe that he hoped someday to find the parts of himself that were lost. Most important, he wanted to recover his brain and his heart so that he could reclaim his memories and share his story with people he cared about.

"I, too, want to know your story, and Nancy and I will help you to discover it," promised Joe. "But now," he said, "I'm anxious to head out and find —"

Joe's sentence and the serenity of the beach were interrupted by a distant, high-pitched, and agonized scream. The arm sprang erect, and Joe froze in horror.

"That was Nancy!" he whispered.

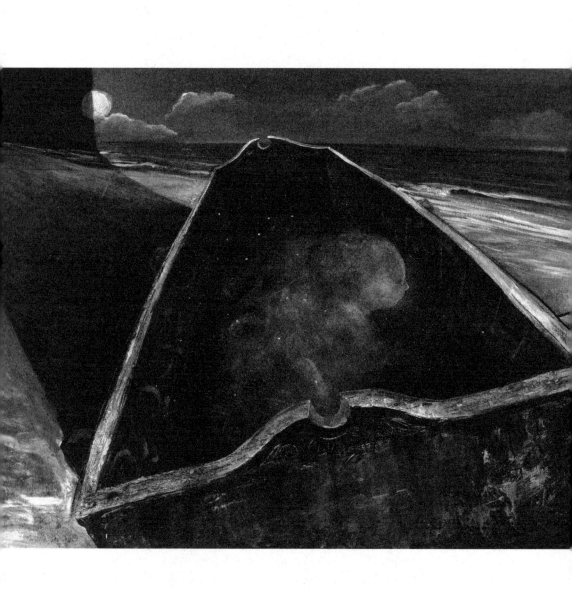

The Shadowy Abyss
of Our Own Fates

♦ ♦ ♦ ♦

Lemony Snicket

illustrated by Timothy Basil Ering

The cradle rocks above an abyss," says an associate of mine, "and common sense tells us that our existence is but a brief crack of light between two eternities of darkness." He is the sort of person who often talks in this sophisticated and somewhat depressing manner, and for that reason he is rarely invited to parties, but he nevertheless makes an important point. Life may seem very long, particularly when you are asked to help put away the groceries, but compared to the vast dark history of the universe, the time from your birth to your death is merely one short blink of light. Even a life story as tumultuous and complicated as that of Nancy and Joe is just a tiny speck in the enormous tumult and complication of life, and if you think too much about this sad, inescapable fact, you are likely to feel like screaming.

This, however, was not the reason Nancy was screaming, which Joe and the robotic arm realized as they staggered over the beach's sand dunes in the direction of her cries. Not fifty feet away to the north, she stood over a small, wavering silhouette. Even as Joe and the arm drew closer, they could not discern what it was. It was shaped something like a boat or perhaps a bed, resting on two upside-down crescent moons like the runners of a rocking chair. But each time the mysterious item moved, it seemed to acquire an enormous shadow — a swath of blackness that made the whole beach as dark and vast as the universe itself. Not until they were standing with Nancy could they see exactly what she was staring at, or why it troubled her so.

It was a cradle, although much bigger than any cradle you've ever slept in unless you were a disturbingly enormous baby, and Nancy was staring into it, her eyes wide with horror, as your mother may have stared into your cradle, one night in your infancy when you thought it was more interesting to scream and cry than to sleep until morning. As the cradle rocked, it cast its tremendous shadow, as far as the children could see, but inside the cradle there was still enough light to see a figure as mysterious as the cradle itself. When the cradle rocked one way, it looked like Baby Max, but each time it moved in the other direction, the baby appeared to melt into the figure of an old man in a tattered tweed suit.

"Is that Baby Max, or something else?" Joe asked his companions, but the robot arm gave a stiff shrug and Nancy shook her head.

"It's trying to talk to us," she said, as the shadow passed over them and then vanished to cast itself on the other side. Sure enough, the melting mouth of the baby or man kept trying to say something, and the twins had to lean in close to the cradle to hear it.

"This is the Cradle of Time," intoned the figure when it was an old man. "It rocks over the abyss of the universe, goo goo ga ga ga."

By the end of the sentence, the cradle had rocked the other way, and the old man had shifted back to infancy and could not talk.

"And who are you?" Nancy asked.

"Goo goo da da Professor Alistair Sloppy, your father," replied the figure. "When I was trying to build an Exquisite

Corpse, I was caught in the mechanics of goo goo ga ga ga ga ga ga, and ended up traveling back in time. But now time has caught up with me, and goo goo goo ga ga wa wa."

"I don't understand," Joe said.

"This journey is almost over, my son," Professor Sloppy said. "This is the closest thing to a sensible explanation that you're going to ga ga ga ga goo goo."

"We've got to get you out of there," Nancy said. "Arm, give me a hand."

"No!" cried Baby Max, using one of the few words he knew. "No, no, Dada climb into the cradle with me. Together we can use it to travel backward or forward in time and ga ga ga ga goo goo."

"We should travel backward," Joe said firmly. "That way, we can stay with our parents and never be orphans, and sort this whole exquisite mess out before it even begins."

"No, we should travel to the future," Nancy said. "That way our entire journey will be over and done with."

The robotic arm moved his palm backward and forward as if to indicate he saw both sides of the issue.

"This is a villainous situation," Joe said. "Who could be behind it? Boppo? Leonardo Dubenski? Genius Kelly? Sybil

Hunch? That monster wolf or that terrible squid? And why? Why are all these villains conspiring against us?"

"I'm beginning to think that there's no reason for all this treachery," Nancy said. "Think of how far we've traveled since that night on the train, and yet our journey is as confusing and mysterious as it ever was. It's as if our lives are being written not by a single, beneficent author, but by a whole team of authors pushing the story every which way, the way an Exquisite Corpse is built from whatever scraps are found." Nancy rested her hand on the robotic hand, who seemed to nod in agreement. "There may be some reason for this journey, but we might not know it until we find ourselves at the end, descending from the Cradle of Time into the shadowy abyss of our own fates."

"You know," Joe said with a gentle smile, "when you talk like this, I worry that you'll never be invited to parties."

Nancy laughed, but the robotic arm gave him a playful shove, accidentally too hard. Joe cried out and began to fall into the crib, grabbing Nancy's arm as he did so. Together the twins tumbled toward the ever-shifting figure of their father, forcing the cradle to fall in the direction the twins had feared most. . . .

Out of the Cradle, Into the Fire

◆ ◆ ◆ ◆ ◆

M. T. Anderson

illustrated by Chris Van Dusen

When the twins opened their eyes, they were in a living room. In a house.

It was a living room like many others, with wall-to-wall carpeting and a plate-glass window and a fake fireplace. But it was unlike many others, because it had been converted into a laboratory. There were all sorts of machines wired to other machines, and someone had written equations in chalk on the floral wallpaper.

"Where are we?" whispered Nancy.

"*When* are we?" Joe wondered.

But there was no time for Nancy to guess before a young couple burst into the room from two opposite doors. The robot arm quivered on Joe's shoulder like a startled parrot.

At first, the young man and woman did not notice the kids. They were in a hurry, carrying duffel bags. The man started grabbing gadgets and devices off tables and throwing them into his bag. The woman was leaning over something on the sofa, wrapping it in a blanket.

And then the man saw them. He straightened up and his eyes narrowed.

"You're invaders," he said. "Aren't you? You've finally come. We'll fight you to the last."

Nancy and Joe gasped. Now that they could see the man's face, they recognized him. He was not as young as his baby self, Max. He was not as old as the old man in the swaying, tragic cradle of time. He was somewhere in the middle. He was about thirty. He had a goatee and wore a tweed suit and viewed them with suspicion. He was their father, Professor Alistair Sloppy. They stared at him in shock.

"Who are you?" Dr. Sloppy demanded.

"Please," said Joe. "We're not invaders." He tried to explain. "We're . . . we're . . ." He held out his hand toward his father.

(His actual hand. Not the one sitting on his shoulder.)

"Honey," said Dr. Sloppy. "We have company."

The young woman turned. She jumped, startled. "Where did they come from?"

Joe and Nancy didn't know what to say.

Nancy said, "We . . . um . . . we came from the circus." Nancy looked at the woman, with her long hair and her many bracelets. Nancy said, "Are you . . . ?" She almost couldn't ask it. She whispered, "Are you Elizabeth Verrie-Sloppy?"

The woman nodded briskly. She said, "Libby Sloppy."

"Libby Sloppy," Nancy repeated, her eyes wide.

"And these," said Libby Sloppy, revealing the swaddled packages on the sofa, "are our twins. Look at them sleeping, Joe and Nancy." Her mouth was sad. "Come on, Alistair," she said to Dr. Sloppy. "We've got to go. We've got to get the babies out of here."

The twin eleven-year-olds looked at the twin babies in awe.

"Joe," repeated Joe softly.

"And Nancy?" said Nancy.

Libby Sloppy nodded again. She raced out of the room. Dr. Sloppy kept throwing equipment in his duffel. "Acrobats from the circus, huh?" said their father. "Well, you've chosen the wrong house to do a double-back somersault into. It's about to be invaded." He said wearily, "We're fleeing."

Nancy and Joe couldn't speak.

They looked at themselves. Their little selves. They were darling as babies. They weren't even a year old. They had sweet little round heads and tiny hands that clamped and unclamped.

Joe said softly, "Was Joe born a little after Nancy? So she's a little bit more old and more boring? And he's younger and more fun?"

Without looking up from his work, Dr. Sloppy said, "They're both wonderful babies." His voice caught. "They're wonderful, wonderful babies. We love them more than anything in the world. And that's why we have to leave them somewhere and flee."

Nancy croaked. "Leave them somewhere?"

Dr. Sloppy was distracted. He spoke without thinking as he pulled plugs out of sockets and disconnected wires from nodes. "I am an inventor," he explained, squinting at some piping. "I invented a doorway into another dimension, so I could travel through time. But the creatures in that dimension—they're angry at me. They're looking for me. Evil. Irascible. Destructifying." He glanced up at the clock.

"They'll be here any minute. We need to vamoose. Abscond. We need to hide these babies somewhere in town." He put down a battery pack and went over to stare at the babies. Tenderly, he murmured, "We have to stash them somewhere they'll be safe, even if their mother and I are caught by the monsters from the other dimension."

Libby Sloppy ran back into the room, twitching her shoulders into a black trench coat. "Come on, Alistair," she said. "No time to cry. We've got to get out of here before the monsters arrive."

Joe had been staring at the scene with his mouth open. Suddenly he twitched as if he'd just awakened. He protested, "You should . . . you should take them with you . . ."

"And love them," said Nancy. "With your whole heart."

The Sloppy parents stopped. They looked at the two kids. "We do," said Dr. Sloppy. "That's why we've got to save them by leaving them somewhere." He shook his head. "If only my father were still around. We could have left them with him." He wiped his eyes. "Oh, Poppy Sloppy," he sighed.

"We haven't even decided yet where we're going to leave them," said Libby. "Where do you think, Alistair? It's time to make up our minds."

Joe and Nancy stared right at her. They felt trapped in the clutch of fate. Joe, as if he were in a trance, said sadly, "You could . . . you could leave them with the circus."

Dr. Alistair Sloppy looked up. "The circus!" he snapped. "Yes! That's a capital idea! The Sick and Tired Circus is in town!"

"Then," said Joe desolately, "they could learn all sorts of skills . . . like knife-throwing . . . and tumbling . . . and lion taming . . . so that maybe someday . . ."

"Maybe," added Nancy miserably, "in ten years . . ."

"They could look for you, and try to save you from the other dimension."

"Because," Nancy finished, "they love you so much, even though they've never met you and don't remember you. But they've thought about you every day of their lives."

Dr. Alistair Sloppy was still busy, spooling wire around his hand. But Libby Sloppy had stopped what she was doing. She was just looking at the kids — the eleven-year-old kids — with wide, startled eyes.

She knew. Nancy and Joe could tell that she knew.

Quietly, she said, "And will those kids be okay? At the Sick and Tired Circus?"

"What's *okay?*" said Joe.

And Nancy answered, "They'll be sad. But there will be really good times, too. Cocoa at night in the fortune-teller's wagon. Playing catch with the elephants. Feeding soup to Decapitata, the Headless Woman. Or at least spooning it into her neck." Nancy went over to her mother's side. Her mother took her hand. Tears were rolling down Nancy's cheeks. "But then some nights, they'll cry into the Bearded Woman's beard."

"What's all this about?" said Dr. Alistair Sloppy impatiently. "Libby, we don't have time to sit here sentimentalizing with whatever pint-size funambulists decide to backflip into our living room in their off-hours. The creatures from the other dimension will be here at any minute, and we'll be mashed into non-Euclidean cud and served for supper." He looked at the kids. "Thank you for your suggestion that we drop the babes off at the circus. We will consider it seriously. Do not worry yourselves about little Joe and Nancy. They will be fine. We have an ally from the other world — a fine pig named Genius Kelly. An interdimensional pig. A porker from beyond the end of time. He'll watch over them."

Looking not at her husband but at Joe and Nancy, Libby Sloppy insisted gently, "The children will make it, won't they? They'll make it, even if their parents — Alistair and me — don't?" She wanted to know the future. Her future. Their future.

Joe said, "Make sure Genius Kelly watches over them real good."

Libby knelt in front of her son. She said, "Is there any other advice I should give Genius Kelly?"

Joe squinted, trying to remember everything that Genius Kelly had told them over the last, kind of confusing, day or two. "Well," he said, "you could suggest that a really good plan would be for Genius Kelly, even though he's on our side, to pretend that he's a bad guy and team up with an evil clown who's trying to kill us, and then Genius Kelly could explain things not by himself but through a hologram of Dr. Albert Einstein that he makes to tell us stuff and to take care of a time-traveled baby Dr. Alistair Sloppy who's on roller skates."

The adult Dr. Alistair Sloppy put down a piece of equipment and looked at Joe, concerned. "*That's* Genius Kelly's plan, you think?" he said.

Joe and Nancy nodded.

Dr. Alistair Sloppy sighed. "Who named that pig Genius?" he asked. Under his breath, he muttered something about interstellar bacon.

He had not even noticed that Joe had said "us" instead of "the babies."

Dr. Alistair Sloppy zipped up his duffel bag. "All right, my stumpy-size circus saltators. Mrs. Sloppy and I have to make ourselves scarce. We have to get these poor darlings off to whatever haven we're planning before —"

"The circus," Libby Sloppy insisted. "Just like these . . . these wonderful, beautiful children suggested. We'll take the babies to the Sick and Tired Circus so they can learn all about how to fight dangers."

Dr. Alistair Sloppy nodded. He struggled into his overcoat. He picked up his duffel bags full of equipment. Libby Sloppy went over and lifted the baby twins, one in each arm.

Then, for a minute, there was one of those strange times that is both heartbreaking and joyous. They stood together as a family for the first time ever, and for the last time in ten years. Dr. Alistair Sloppy didn't know it yet, of course. He just thought Nancy and Joe were circus acrobats. But Libby Sloppy did know it. She had tears in her eyes, because she was leaving behind not two of her children but four. And that moment there in the house, waiting for creatures to invade from another dimension, had to stand in for all those other moments the four of them had missed together, and would miss, over the next ten years — the twins running home from the bus after the first day of school . . . making construction-paper masks on long Saturday afternoons . . . scribbling in crayon on the walls . . . telling on each other in the back-seat during car rides to national parks . . . standing before the Grand Canyon with their father, Alistair Sloppy, taking snaps with an interdimensional camera that photographed not just the kids and the mother and the mesas but also the glimmerings of light from other worlds, the many-eyed beings floating past invisibly in the desert air.

None of those things would happen. Not, at least, until a decade had passed.

So they stood for one last time, six and a quarter people who formed a family of four.

(The quarter is the arm.)

And then the house began to shake.

"They're coming!" cried Dr. Sloppy, wading toward the front door, his duffel bags clanking.

The house rattled. The windows wobbled.

"What?" said Joe. "Who's coming?"

"The creatures from the other dimension!" said Libby

Sloppy. She jerked her head toward the door. "Come on!" she exclaimed. "Come on, kids."

Joe and Nancy looked at each other. They looked at the two babies, swaddled in their mother's arms.

And Joe bravely stepped forward. "No," he said. "You go. We're going to stay here. We'll delay the monsters to give you time to get away."

Libby Sloppy looked at them like they were crazy. "You can't stay."

But Nancy stepped forward and stood by Joe. She shook her head. "We have to stay here. Someone's got to make sure that those . . . those babies are safe. They've got to have a chance to get to the circus. So that they can have, you know, their whole future."

Libby Sloppy looked at Nancy and Joe with pleading eyes. "Kids . . ." she whispered.

Dr. Sloppy smiled at them. "Thank you," he said. "You're wonderful children, to intervene this way." He clanked back to Joe's side and mussed up Joe's hair a little. "If we elude the monsters, we'll come back and check up on you," he said. "I promise."

The kids blinked with tears in their eyes. The house

vibrated. Some plates toppled over in the kitchen and crashed. "All right," said Dr. Alistair Sloppy, and he headed out.

"Wait!" Joe cried. "But what *are* the monsters? What do they look like?"

"Anything they want to!" Dr. Alistair Sloppy called from the front door. "A tree! A wolf! A clown! Anything in the world!"

Libby Sloppy explained, "Their true form is —"

"No time!" said Dr. Alistair Sloppy. "They're almost here! Come along!" And then their father was gone.

"Good-bye! Good-bye, my darlings!" said Libby Sloppy, right behind him. She stood for a moment. The door frame jiggled as the beasts approached from their dimension. Then, with wet eyes, she turned away and ran into the night.

Nancy looked after her, wanting to wail.

But there was no time to wail. Joe was already bustling around, thinking of things he could flip and throw at the monsters. "All right," he said. "We have to be prepared. We have the skills." He rushed off into another room.

Nancy started looking around the living-room laboratory for something that might delay monsters. She knew enough from assisting magicians that she could make explosions and puffs of smoke, if she could find the right stuff. She gathered together bottles of chemicals.

Not enough. She couldn't find the right ingredients. She yelled to her brother, "Did you find anything in there, Joe?"

"Naw," he called back. "Just a tank."

"A tank?!?" Nancy said. "Like a *shooting* tank?"

"No. Not really a tank. A trunk."

"A trunk?!? What's in it? Open it!"

"Not that kind of trunk. I mean, like the trunk of a body. A torso. You know, made of metal, with rivets. Like a round water tank, but with holes for legs and a head and — oh — oh! For arms!"

Nancy looked up.

Arms.

Both of them had found an arm recently.

So . . . two robot arms and a torso.

"The Exquisite Corpse's body!" Joe exclaimed. "This must be the robot's trunk!"

Nancy was already racing into the bedroom to see what Joe was talking about.

Joe knelt by the tank, or the trunk. It was blackened

from some explosion, but it was clearly the body of a robot with no head and no legs. Arm was skipping around happily. Joe was trying to screw Arm into the socket. "Stop it!" he said. "Stop dancing!"

Nancy rushed to the other side of the trunk. She examined the socket on the body. She hefted the dead robot arm she'd found near the pirate. She started to screw the arm in.

The house shook harder. The invaders were coming. Plaster cracked. A window shattered.

The two kids had fixed the arms into the metal body.

They stood up. They watched. They didn't know what to do.

Pictures fell off the walls. On the other side of the door, there was a *zap*.

And then something was in the living-room laboratory, just down the hall. Something was breathing.

Nancy and Joe looked at each other in horror.

And by their knees, glinting dully, the legless, headless robot began to move.

SKILLS

◆ ◆ ◆ ◆

LINDA SUE PARK

illustrated by JAMES RANSOME

A raspy voice scraped the air. "I'll get you, Nancy and Joe," it said, "and your little robot, too."

The voice had come from the living room, down the hall from the bedroom where the twins were now.

"It's the wolf!" Joe whispered, his eyes wide. His hand went automatically to the pocket of his trousers. The key was still there — the key he had worked so hard to recover after they had lost it during their earlier encounter with the wolf. "We gotta get out of here! We have to get back to the cradle!"

They had already seen it outside the living-room window — the giant Cradle of Time that had brought them here to the past, to the house where they were born. To reach the cradle, they would have to get by the wolf.

Nancy clutched at her forearm, which seemed to be pulsing strongly. It wasn't painful, but it reminded her of how the wolf's claws had scratched her deeply, drawing blood. The odd thing was —

"Nancy, look!" Joe pointed at the robot. "It's booting up!"

Lights were flashing on the robot's torso. It began humming, then emitted a string of buzzes and beeps.

Supporting itself on its hands, the headless robot swung its torso forward. Hands — torso — hands — torso. . . . About the height of a sturdy three-year-old, it "walked" around the room, covering ground quite nicely and beeping as it went. Joe thought it seemed delighted to be able to move. Well, as delighted as a torso and two arms could be.

"It can already walk — just think how smart it will be once we've found all of it!" Nancy exclaimed.

Their joy was short-lived, for now they could hear the wolf in the living room, opening and closing closet and cupboard doors, slobbering, slavering, panting. . . .

Nancy thought hard. It was strange, almost as if she could sense what the wolf was thinking. Then, "I have an idea," she said. "We have to get to the kitchen."

Joe picked up the robot. "C'mon, buddy," he said.

"How do you know it's a boy?" Nancy asked. She was beginning to feel annoyed at the paltry number of females in this adventure. "I think it's a girl. I'm going to call it"—she paused and looked at the robot appraisingly—"Roberta. Roberta the robot. Hi, Roberta."

The robot waved its arms with such enthusiasm that Joe had to duck out of the way.

"See? She likes her name," Nancy said.

Joe frowned. "You think she heard that?"

He set the robot down and examined it quickly. On the front panel he found a small microphone grille.

"She booted up when we got both arms in," Joe said thoughtfully, "and now it looks like she *can* actually hear us."

"Cool!" Nancy said, and Roberta let loose a cheerful whistle.

"Okay, let's go," Joe said, and picked up Roberta again. He was glad that the robot had a torso now. Already he was missing Baby Max, who had transformed into an adult while in the giant cradle. Into Dr. Alistair Sloppy.

Dad.

Dad and Mom had hurriedly left the house with two infants — Nancy and Joe themselves, in the past. It had been beyond frustrating for the twins to see their parents for such a short time before being separated again. And if putting together the Exquisite Corpse was the way to reunite them once and for all, then nothing else was more important.

The trio slipped out the door and down the hall. Joe glanced fearfully over his shoulder; any minute now, the wolf was bound to leave the living room.

In the kitchen, Nancy rifled through the refrigerator. She pulled out a chicken and a whole salami.

"Nancy! I'm hungry, too, but we don't have time to eat!"

"I need just one more thing," she said, still rummaging. "Well, this isn't ideal, but it'll have to do." She began unwrapping a package of ground beef.

"What the —?"

"Did you hear all that slobbering?" Nancy said. "It's hungry. I'm betting it will be more interested in this food than in us — at least for a few seconds. And it's not stealing, because, technically, this is our house, right?"

"You have a plan?"

Nancy's eyes began to glow a little; she was almost smiling. They held a quick conference, their voices low.

"What about your arm?" Joe asked anxiously.

"Oh — I was going to tell you before! Look." Nancy pushed up her sleeve to show Joe the wound.

It was completely healed, with only a faint shadow of a line where the scratch had been.

Joe was amazed. "How did it get better so fast?"

Nancy shook her head. "I don't know. That ride in the cradle, somehow?" She didn't mention that if anything, her arm felt even stronger than usual now. Maybe it was just her imagination. . . .

There was no time to speculate further. "Ready?" Nancy said. "One, two, three, shoot."

They played three rounds of rock-paper-scissors to determine who would leave the room first. Joe tried to outthink his sister. She always threw paper last. But he knew that she knew that he knew she always threw paper last, so he thought she would think he was thinking exactly that and would therefore throw something different.

Joe threw rock.

Nancy threw paper.

"Dang it!" Joe exclaimed.

But losing at rock-paper-scissors was soon to be the least of his problems.

Joe took a deep breath and tiptoed into the front hall. Roberta followed him dutifully.

"Shh," he whispered. The robot let out one last little *bip* and went silent.

The wolf spotted the boy and the robot, and calmly padded over to stand between them and the door that led outside.

"Why, Joe," it rasped. "I was just thinking about you."

Its prey trapped, the wolf was in no hurry. It licked its lips menacingly. Its yellow eyes narrowed into a sneer, and it took a couple of slow, arrogant steps toward Joe.

Joe felt his nerve crumbling like a cookie in cocoa. *I hope it doesn't tear me limb from limb,* he thought. *If I have to die like this, a good hard bite to the spinal cord first would be best — that way I wouldn't feel anything more. . . .*

The wolf crouched, ready to spring.

Joe's breath caught and he cowered against the wall. "Uh, Nancy?" he croaked. "Anytime now?"

Nancy stepped out of the kitchen, her arms full. "Hey!" she hollered at the wolf defiantly. "What about me?"

She didn't even need to glance at Joe; she knew he'd be ready. How many times had they done this routine? Hundreds of times. No, thousands. Balls, clubs, hoops, platters. On the ground, on tightrope, on horseback. On a trampoline, on the shoulders of other performers. They'd even juggled blind-folded. They could have done the routine in their sleep: cascade, reverse cascade, shower, back cross, shoulder throw, repeat, repeat, repeat, finish with a Mills Mess, curtsy, bow.

On second thought, maybe they would save the curtsy and bow for later.

Nancy started the cascade and then began feeding Joe. The chicken and the salami, despite the differences in their weights and shapes, were working out nicely. In fact, the salami was a piece of cake.

The ground beef, however, was less cooperative.

Nancy had packed the beef into a ball as best she could, but it started to disintegrate almost immediately. Clumps of ground beef flew through the air. Some landed on the floor while others stuck to the walls and the ceiling. With each toss, there was less beef to work with, and Joe began to worry that they wouldn't make it to the back cross.

His fears were groundless. Nancy's plan was working! Distracted by the smell of raw meat and addled by trying to keep its eye on both the food and the children, the wolf began leaping and snapping at the bits of beef that were flying about. Joe edged his way toward the door, still juggling the chicken and the salami and the woebegone little wad of beef that remained.

"Now!" Nancy yelled.

Roberta reached out and, after a couple of groping attempts — she couldn't see, of course — located the doorknob and threw open the door. Joe scooped up the robot and ran. Nancy hurled the chicken and the salami at the wolf as hard as she could, then raced out the door and slammed it behind her.

The cradle was directly over the front lawn. Not *on* the lawn, but hovering in the air ten or twelve feet above it.

"Human chain!" Joe shouted. He hurried to position himself beneath one of the cradle's giant rockers and went down on one knee. Nancy was on his shoulders in a flash. Joe stood up and took Roberta by the hand.

"Alley-oop!" Joe swung the robot up toward Nancy, who caught the other hand.

"Oh, dear," Nancy said. "How are we going to do this? She doesn't have any legs!"

Roberta let go of Joe's hand and whistled electronically, waving her arm in big circles.

"Hey! Cut it out!" Joe yelled, staggering a little.

Roberta stilled her arm immediately and let out a couple of apologetic-sounding beeps. A series of mechanical, electrical, and hydraulic sounds ensued as the robot busily maneuvered herself until she was doing a one-armed handstand on top of Nancy's head. She was now high enough to grab the cradle's rocker with her free hand.

Just then, the wolf burst out the door, chomping on the last of the salami.

"Joe! Grab my ankles!" Nancy yelled. He obeyed immediately.

Nancy reached up and hung on to Roberta's arm for dear life. More noises: clanking, cranking, straining sounds, as Roberta began hauling up her heavy burden.

Joe's feet were now dangling a few yards above the ground. The wolf leapt into the air. Joe kicked out as hard as he could, hitting the wolf's muzzle. The cradle lurched. Nancy screamed, and the wolf circled around below them, ready for another attack.

Roberta emitted a series of noises that alternated

between a siren and a blast of microphone feedback. It was deafening; the wolf put its head on the ground and held its ears.

Then Roberta began to swing the arm that Nancy was holding. Back and forth, back and forth, slowly at first, then faster and harder. The twins fishtailed wildly through the air.

"YOWWWWW!" yelled one twin, and "YIIIIKES!" yelled the other.

"Roberta, what are you DOING?" Nancy shrieked as she tried to tighten her grip.

Joe had a sudden flash of insight. "Nancy — it's okay! I get what she's trying to do! Just hang on and think trapeze!"

"Oh oh oh!"

When Roberta had built up enough momentum, she gave a final, mighty swing. Joe and Nancy soared in an arc with Roberta as its fulcrum. At the height of the arc, when they were directly above the cradle, Roberta let go of them.

Nancy and Joe landed in a heap in the cradle, which fortunately had a nice cushy mattress topped by a down comforter. As they caught their breath after their wild ride, Roberta pulled herself up over the edge of the cradle and tumbled in next to them.

Beep-beep-bip-bip-beep? she asked.

Nancy couldn't help but laugh. "We're okay, Roberta. How about you?"

Before Roberta could beep a reply, the cradle began to rock, and all three of them slid to one side. The cradle tipped so far that they had to hold on to each other and anything else they could reach.

When at last they leveled out again, the cradle stopped moving. Cautiously, Joe stood up and peeked over the edge.

They were on the beach again — exactly as they had left it.

Back in the present.

THE GINGERBREAD HOUSE

✦ ✦ ✦ ✦

KATHERINE PATERSON

illustrated by CALEF BROWN

Well, Nancy, here we are again — the same old beach that we left behind. Was it hours ago? Or days ago?"

"It's felt like weeks," said Nancy. "Weeks without any sleep."

"Or food," said Joe.

"What about Baby Max's lunch?" asked Nancy, trying not to sound as prickly as she felt. She remembered quite well the sight of Baby Max, Genius Kelly, and Joe pigging out on the contents of that blue plastic *Star Wars* lunch box and then had to immediately apologize mentally for pigism to Genius Kelly, who really was a pig and might well be sensitive. Fortunately, no one had heard this moral lapse. She was wondering if it might have something to do with having been scratched by that horrible wolf when she realized that she should have been listening to her brother instead of thinking only of herself.

"That was days ago," Joe was saying, "and besides, the thermos was missing. I haven't had a drop to drink since we dived into the river."

"What about when you were under the sea?"

"Nancy! Surely you know that you mustn't drink seawater. You would die of thirst after all that salt."

Nancy was a bit embarrassed to be reminded of this simple scientific fact. After all, she was the elder by ninety seconds and universally acknowledged as mentally as well as morally superior to her delightful, fun-loving, younger brother. She decided to change the subject. "It's getting dark, Joe. Why don't we take shelter under those trees at the edge of the woods and go to sleep? Everything will seem clearer in the morning."

You would think that after all the bad surprises of this adventure, the twins would have been terrified to close their eyes, but they reckoned there was a Saline Solution Sea between them and the Leonardo Dubenski band of villains; the wolf was trapped in another dimension; the giant squid was deep under the brine; and Boppo, well, knowing the clown's problems with staying awake, he was probably snoring away somewhere under his own tree.

Nevertheless, Joe and Nancy snuggled up close to Roberta's torso, and the robot put one electronic arm around each of them and gently beeped a lullaby to the weary pair.

Toward dawn a snorting sort of snore jolted Joe wide awake. Boppo? The evil clown was forever turning up at the most awkward moments, and he was a first-class snorer. Joe was quite sure that he'd never heard Nancy snore and that robots surely didn't. He sat up cautiously. A few feet beyond Roberta and Nancy was a rising and falling hump of something snorting like a steam engine with each breath.

"Psst, Nancy," he whispered. "Wake up. We've got company."

But Nancy only sighed and snuggled closer to Roberta.

Joe stood up and peered more closely at the noisy lump. In the early morning light he was able to make out, to his great relief, not Boppo, but the sleek black form of Genius Kelly.

"Humph," said Joe. "Some guardian you turned out to

be." There was no answer from the pig, unless you count a wheezy snuffle from a snoring snout. "Yeah, one super body-guard," he said disgustedly, and as he looked he seemed to see imposed on the prone body a diagram from the butcher shop indicating hock, pork belly, loin chop, ham. . . . His mouth was watering. He forced himself to turn away from such disloyal thoughts. What would his parents think of him if they knew he was regarding as potential bacon the extraterrestrial help they had sent the twins?

He sat down again as close to Roberta as possible. Where could they find something to eat? There was no sign of civilization in this desolate place, with the Saline Solution Sea in one direction and dark woods in the other. Of course, the most important thing was to find Roberta's missing head and legs, but surely they couldn't keep up the search with nothing to eat or drink.

It was then that he thought of Sybil Hunch. Of all the people and creatures they'd encountered, with the exception, of course, of Genius Kelly and the pirate Angel, the misfortune-teller had seemed, if not an ally, at least not an enemy. Hadn't she changed the ropes that Leonardo Dubenski had bound them with into ivy? He didn't relish the thought of arm wrestling the giant squid again, even aided by a two-armed Roberta, but Genius Kelly was here now. He had obviously found a way around the sea. He could lead them back that way and help them find Sybil Hunch's house. She was a woman, he thought, like the bearded lady, who was a terrific cook.

When Nancy finally woke up, she was so happy to see Genius Kelly that she ran over and shook him awake. He was not pleased, but he stiffly allowed a hug around his belly, trying to maintain his dignity.

"Where were you all this time?" Joe asked, remembering all that had happened since they'd last seen the pig.

"That's not what I'd regard as a warm welcome," the pig said huffily. "It was a long way around the sea."

"Sorry," said Joe, none too graciously, "but I haven't had anything to eat for days, so I'm feeling pretty grumpy. I think, however, I know where we can get some breakfast." But when Joe shared his plan, neither Nancy nor the pig was enthusiastic.

"Too many nettles along the route," grumbled the pig.

"You remember what happened the last time we ran into the Dubenski gang," Nancy said. "I'm hungry, too, Joe, but we can't just go off on our own. We have to follow the arrows. With everything that's been going on, we haven't even had a chance to consult them." Then, looking at Joe's crest-fallen face, she added, "Maybe they'll point us toward food and drink as well as Roberta's missing parts. That's the most important thing, Joe. We have to find the rest of Roberta."

Roberta gave a few affirmative beeps — not so many as to seem interfering, but just enough to show where she would stand, if she had a leg to stand on.

Joe sighed, but he took off his shoe and examined the arrow on his little toe. Meanwhile, Nancy and Genius Kelly were examining theirs as well.

There was no arguing. All three arrows pointed in the same direction — straight into the woods.

Nancy tried once more to cheer Joe up. "Maybe we'll find berries along the way," she said.

Joe smiled weakly. She was a brave girl, that sister of his. There was nothing to do but heave Roberta under his arm and follow Nancy and the pig straight in between the dark overhanging branches of the trees.

They had been trudging along for what seemed liked hours when Joe stopped in his tracks. "What's that smell?" His alert nose had picked up a delicious aroma. The little band pressed forward, forgetting arrows, forgetting fear, forgetting everything, I am sorry to say, but their empty tummies.

Just ahead of them in a clearing, the noonday sun shone down on a tiny house. It had two chimneys, and smoke was definitely coming out of one of them, as was the wonderful aroma.

"Food!" Joe said, and, forgetting all caution, started to run toward the house, but Nancy, her arm that had been scratched by the wolf strangely strong, reached out and grabbed her brother, holding him fast.

"Joe, wait! I think—I think that cottage is made of gingerbread."

"All the better," said Joe. "Gingerbread for breakfast!"

"But, Joe, don't you remember the story?"

"What story?"

Nancy opened her mouth to answer, but at that exact moment, Roberta began to wriggle under Joe's arm. The twins watched openmouthed in amazement. When she was nearly upright, she swung her arm up toward the roof of the little house and began beeping frantically.

Two children and a pig looked up to see what this anxious signal might mean. Could it be? Yes. The second chimney looked strangely like an upside-down leg.

IF I ONLY HAD A LEG

✦ ✦ ✦ ✦

KATE DiCAMILLO

illustrated by TIMOTHY BASIL ERING

In fact, it was a leg.

And surely it was Roberta's leg. It must be. Because things always work out in the end, don't they? Missing parts are found. Siblings are reunited. Parents return from another dimension. That's how stories move along: from chaos to happily ever after. That's the *point* of a story.

Usually.

"Oh, Roberta," said Nancy. "I'm so happy for you. The happiest days are always the days when missing legs are found. Aren't they, Joe? Aren't those the happiest days?"

Joe didn't answer.

"Joe?" said Nancy.

Nancy looked away from the glittering, beckoning chimney/robot leg only to find that Joe and Genius Kelly were engaged in a shocking act of vandalism. They were *eating* the gingerbread house.

"Stop," said Nancy. "Stop it right now, both of you!"

"But it's good," said Joe.

"It's not the best gingerbread I've ever had," said Genius Kelly. "It's too salty. I'm afraid that 'edible' is the highest compliment I can bestow upon it. And even that might be a bit of a stretch."

"I think it's great!" said Joe. He was shoving huge chunks of a gingerbread windowsill into his mouth and swallowing without even bothering to chew. Such greed! Such hunger! Nancy found it disagreeable. Her stomach, however, was not as principled. It growled in jealousy.

"Both of you should stop eating," she said. "One, it's rude to eat someone's house. Two, haven't you ever read *Hansel and Gretel*?"

"Read who and who?" said Genius Kelly. It was obvious that the pig's inherent pigginess was winning out over his honor, his commitment to his sacred duty of guarding Nancy and Joe. It was frightening to Nancy to see how one's baser nature could so easily come to the fore.

"Please stop," said Nancy.

Joe shoved more gingerbread into his mouth. He swallowed. "I think there's some even better food inside. I can smell it. It smells like, um . . ." He put his nose up in the air and sniffed. His chin was covered in crumbs. His nose twitched. "Meatballs," said Joe. He nodded. He burped.

"Did someone say 'meatballs'?" said a voice that was funny but not that funny.

The door to the gingerbread house swung open.

A clown stepped out. He was wearing floral-patterned oven mitts on both his hands.

"Boppo!" said Nancy.

"Bbbpp," said Joe, spraying crumbs everywhere.

Would the Sloppy twins ever truly shed their circus past? More to the point: would they ever truly rid their life of clowns?

"You sorry excuse for a —" said Genius Kelly.

And then, midsentence, the pig fell right off his four cloven feet and onto his side.

"Genius Kelly!" said Nancy. Was he dead? Could it be?

The pig started to snore.

"Oook," said Joe, his mouth too full for proper speech. He pointed with a chunk of gingerbread house at the pig. He laughed. "Eee afleep!" And with those words (or whatever they were), Joe, too, fell from his feet onto the forest floor and descended directly into a peaceful, unconcerned slumber of his own.

Boppo laughed. He clapped his oven mitts together. "Sometimes," he said, "if the gingerbread is spiced correctly, wonderful, magical things can happen."

"You drugged the gingerbread?" said Nancy.

"Yes," said Boppo. He smiled at Nancy. His lips were very, very red. "Dearie," he said.

And that one word, that one insincere endearment, was truly chilling to hear. The very forest trembled with the sound of it. The world grew still.

A lone, brave bird sang.

Genius Kelly snored.

And from inside the gingerbread house, an oven timer dinged.

"Ooop," said Boppo. "The meatballs are ready. Back in a jiff."

The clown disappeared. Nancy ran over to Joe. She

knelt down and slapped his face gently. And then she slapped it not so gently.

"Wake up," she said. "Joe, please. Wake up." Joe had an idiotic, carefree smile plastered on his face. It was annoying.

Nancy turned to the pig and slapped him just for the satisfaction of slapping someone.

Boppo returned. He stood over Nancy with his oven-mitted hands on his hips.

"Terrible disease, narcolepsy," he said. "You never know when it's going to strike next. And hey, Nancy, can I just say that you seem to have left your precious robot untended?"

Roberta! Nancy had forgotten all about her. She turned. Roberta was sitting on the forest floor. Both her arms were raised above her torso. She was reaching for her leg, which was perched high above her on the roof of the gingerbread house.

The robot let out a sad toot. To be so close to one of her missing parts and yet unable to reach it had obviously unhinged her. She was diminished, undone, frozen into immobility by her longing. And to Nancy, it suddenly seemed untenable that everything depended on a few pieces of mangled metal named Roberta.

But everything did depend on her.

Nancy eyed Boppo.

Boppo eyed Nancy.

And then they both sprinted toward Roberta. Boppo got there first. No one ever thinks that clowns are fast, but they are excessively speedy. Deceptively so.

Boppo clutched Roberta's torso to his chest. "Mine," he said. "All mine. And soon to be no more, for I will disassemble her."

"No," said Nancy. "Give her back!"

"Ha!" said Boppo. "I've got a better idea. Why don't you come inside and have a meatball and we'll read some poetry and then you can watch while I take your robot apart?"

"Are you kidding?" said Nancy.

This was a rhetorical question.

But, really, what choice did Nancy have?

This is not a rhetorical question.

It's an actual question. I want you to answer it. She could have walked away, of course. She could have abandoned her sleeping brother and the worthless pig. She could have left the half-assembled robot to her fate of being taken apart entirely. But then the mystery would be unsolved, the corpse unassembled, her parents unfound.

Also, it wouldn't be moral.

And so Nancy went into the house of the clown and sat with a plate of meatballs (they smelled delicious, but who knew what kind of Boppo poison they contained) in her lap while Boppo read aloud to her from his tattered copy of the collected poems of Edna St. Vincent Millay.

Roberta, in her reduced state, seemed to enjoy the poems. Rumbles and toots and whistles emanated from her torso, but Nancy was too distracted to derive much pleasure from poetry.

How could she get Roberta's leg off the roof? More to the point: how could she stop Boppo from taking Roberta apart entirely? How could she, Nancy, work to put things together? Would Joe ever wake up? Did she really care if Genius Kelly ever woke up? Man, she was hungry; should she eat a meatball? These were the questions that bedeviled her.

Meanwhile, Boppo was reading a poem called "The Ballad of the Harp-Weaver." It was a very long poem, and Boppo was crying as he read it. Big, fat tears rolled through his white clown makeup and left streaks of pink skin behind. His hair was, of course, standing on end, and the book of Ms. Millay's poems looked very small and pathetic clutched in Boppo's big oven mitts.

Oh, thought Nancy, *sometimes the world is too ridiculous to be borne.*

And then, suddenly, Boppo stopped reading.

The poem was over!

No, even better: the clown was asleep.

"Ha!" said Nancy. She stood up. She put down the plate of meatballs. And without any moral agonizing at all, she bent to the sleeping clown and emptied his pockets. He was a shockingly predictable clown: red rubber nose, red rubber nose, brown rubber rat, another red rubber nose. A meatball. Another red rubber nose. No, wait. This nose was different. It pulsed. It glowed. It wasn't rubber and it wasn't a nose. Nancy held the red, glowing thing aloft.

Beside her, Roberta's torso came to life. The robot chirped and sang. Her arms waved back and forth. She emanated hope. And Nancy suddenly realized what she held in her hand. It was the robot's heart.

"Why, with a heart and a torso and two arms and one leg, there's nowhere you can't go, Roberta," said Nancy. "All things are possible now."

A shadow darkened the doorway of the gingerbread house. Dear Joe. Reliable Joe. He was awake. They would put Roberta together. It would all work out!

But it was not Joe. Oh, no. This shadow belonged to another.

SPEAK, MEMORY

✦ ✦ ✦ ✦

SUSAN COOPER

illustrated by CHRIS VAN DUSEN

Nancy looked at the huge shadow blotting out the golden light of sunset in the doorway, and felt cold with foreboding. What was it? She had to act without Joe, right this minute.

Beside her, the little robot was now waving her arms up and down, beeping urgently. Nancy caught one of the arms, and into its hand she put the glowing red robotic heart that she had rescued from Boppo's pocket. Roberta's beeps became a wild medley of joyful chirps, and she opened a little square door in her metal chest and popped the heart inside.

Then she began to purr. It was a sound rather like an electric fan.

But from outside the gingerbread house, Nancy could hear a deeper purring, more like a diesel motor, accompanied by a kind of muted clapping. She stood stock-still. Was it possible? These had been the happiest sounds of her life ever since she was a baby. She began to smile, feeling her own heart pounding with excitement. She ran through the door and looked upward, beaming.

"Oh, Hathi!" she said joyfully. "It's you! It's really you!"

And there stood the twins' beloved foster mother from the Sick and Tired Circus, all seven thousand pounds of her. It was Hathi the elephant, rumbling and flapping her ears with pleasure as she nosed at Joe's sleeping form with the tip of her trunk. The trunk rose into the air and descended gently on Nancy's face in a happy greeting; it was like being kissed by the hose of a vacuum cleaner.

Nancy cried tears of mingled joy and guilt and relief. After that life-changing moment at the Elephant Clown Party, when they had been forced to leave without a word of farewell, she had despaired of ever seeing Hathi again.

"I'm so glad to see you!" she wept. "We just had to go — it was when he gave us the card —"

"Never mind," said Hathi. "Your secret circus support system kept me informed." She raised her trunk again, dipped it into a sturdy box strapped to her back, and presented Nancy with a large, perfectly ripe banana.

"You look hungry, my darling," she said.

"Oh, thank you!" Nancy's tears gave way to famished gratitude.

Joe stirred, and opened his eyes.

"Hathi!" he cried, and he leapt to his feet. Love can work wonders; it beats drugged gingerbread every time.

Nancy stroked Hathi's trunk. "You came after us!" she said through a mouthful of banana.

"Well, I knew that witless pig would screw things up," said Hathi, with a withering glance at the sleeping Genius Kelly. "He's so full of himself! All these contradictory stories — you need support, not a firework display. I know just where you should go next, on this perilous journey. And I've arrived only just in time — I smell danger!"

Her long trunk swung to and fro and paused at the doorway of the gingerbread house. "I smell *Boppo!*" said Hathi in a terrible voice.

"Is he in there?" said Joe sleepily to Nancy.

Nancy glared at him. "If you hadn't been gobbling up

his gingerbread, you'd know that! Let's get out of here!" Then she froze. "But we need Roberta!"

She dashed into the house, with Joe stumbling after her. The tip of Hathi's trunk hovered in the doorway.

There was the little robot, armed but legless, still purring — but she had her arms around the sleeping Boppo.

Joe tugged at her. "Roberta! Come quick!"

Roberta clung more tightly. She purred more loudly.

"She has feelings now," Nancy said. "She has a heart! I emptied Boppo's pockets and there it was."

"So she's fallen in love with *Boppo?*" said Joe. "Where's her common sense?" He sighed, and shook his head. "I wish you'd found her brain instead."

"Hmm," said Nancy. "I wonder . . ."

She turned to look at the contents of Boppo's pockets, still scattered over the floor. Hathi's trunk was already there, sensitive, groping. It picked up one of the red rubber noses and held it out to Nancy.

Roberta stopped purring, and let go of Boppo.

Nancy took the nose and shook it over her palm. Out fell a tiny piece of green metal patterned with a maze of gleaming lines. Roberta uttered some rapid, urgent chirps and waved her arms.

"It looks very electronic," said Nancy. "It must be her brain!" She dropped it into Roberta's hand.

Joe said, "But we haven't found her head yet!"

Roberta opened the small square door in her chest and slid her brain into a waiting slot, to join her heart. She said, in a beautifully modulated Oxford English accent, "It is deeply anthropomorphic to assume that a robot must necessarily require a head."

On the floor, Boppo stirred.

Everyone held their breath.

Boppo licked his very, very red lips. "More meatballs!" he said sleepily.

Roberta's little robotic arms moved like lightning. They broke off a piece of the gingerbread windowsill, crumbled it, and popped the morsels rapidly one by one into Boppo's mouth. He chewed contentedly. "Mmmm," he said.

It was several seconds before his taste buds told him he wasn't eating meatballs, and his eyes flickered in alarm — but it was too late. He was fast asleep again.

"Hoist with his own petard," said Roberta with satisfaction.

Joe said, "Is she going to talk like this all the time?"

"Out!" said Nancy. She paused, added politely, "Excuse

me, Roberta," and thrust the little robot into Hathi's curling trunk, following it outside.

"A pleasure to meet you, proud pachyderm," said Roberta's diminishing voice as she was swung high into the air, "and if I could trouble you to divert a little leftward — a little more — *yes!*"

They saw her eager mechanical arms clutch the chimney leg — and then saw it crumble. It wasn't a robotic leg after all; it was just gingerbread, pretending.

"Rats!" said Roberta, and she disappeared, as Hathi's trunk swung her over to the howdah (a fancy name for the box, which was indeed pretty fancy) on her back. Then the trunk came down again, tip curved, and with the skill of lifelong practice, Nancy and Joe stepped aboard. They rose through the air just as they had at the circus: feet standing on the tip of Hathi's trunk, hands against the trunk itself, for balance. It was their favorite form of travel in the world, ending with a small acrobatic leap into the howdah.

The instant they were safely on her back, the great gray elephant went striding away through the trees. And Nancy, Joe, and Roberta found that they were not alone.

"There's a whole hand of bananas under your seat," said

a voice. "Hathi always had a strong maternal instinct, even if they did give her a male name."

Sitting on one of the padded, velvet-covered seats, next to Roberta, was an old lady in a black cloak, with frizzy white hair escaping around her hood like an ermine trim. It was Sybil Hunch, eating a banana.

"We're so glad to see you, Miss Hunch," said Nancy, wondering whether this was true. She felt they had had enough misfortunes already without having more predicted.

"When an old friend calls, I come," said Sybil Hunch. "Hathi and I go back a ways — I was a member of your circus once. Long before your time. But the public isn't very partial to misfortune-tellers."

Joe reached for the bananas; even after the gingerbread, he was still hungry. The howdah was swaying vigorously now as Hathi loped through the forest. The sun had set, and in the dying light they could see Sybil Hunch's crystal ball in her lap, gleaming faintly.

"We love Hathi," Joe said, chewing. "She raised us, more than anyone else in the circus."

"She's our mother," Nancy said simply. "Or she was, until the ringmaster gave us that card from our real parents.

At seven o'clock on our eleventh birthday, the way they'd told him to. And we had to run for that terrible train."

"Right in the middle of our birthday party," Joe said. "The elephants and the clowns gave us a party every year — a competition, to see which of them could make us laugh the hardest. They'd only just begun." He sniffed mournfully.

Nancy said, "We're doing what the card told us. We're hunting for every piece of the Exquisite Corpse — that's Roberta — so we can rescue our parents. But it gets harder all the time!"

"Well, now," said Sybil Hunch. "Let's see if the past can throw any light on the future." She tossed her banana peel overboard and gave her crystal ball a quick rub with the edge of her cloak.

"Memory search," she said crisply to the ball. "Sloppy twins, background of."

They peered over her shoulder as the ball filled with whirling mist, and they saw a flurry of images. First they saw their youthful father and mother with Roberta, as she opened a door into another dimension; then the evil, irascible, destructifying creatures snarling at their parents from the other side of the door. The mist swirled, and they saw the Sloppys hastily push the door closed. At the very last moment, one of the creatures dived out after them: a form-less monster, pursued by a bright dancing light. Then they saw Roberta's metal hand turn a key in the door's lock.

"What's that light?" said Joe, peering.

"Beneficence, I'd guess," said Sybil Hunch. "Hush. Watch."

"Joe!" whispered Nancy. "Have you still got that key?"

Joe nodded, and Sybil Hunch said, "*Hush!*"

They saw Alistair Sloppy handing his small, adorable babies to the circus ringmaster, together with a sealed envelope. The ringmaster was nodding his head seriously. An elephant was dimly visible in the background. Panning to another part of the circus, the crystal ball showed them the monster morphing into the body of Boppo the clown.

Joe hissed. So did Roberta.

"HUSH!" said Nancy and Sybil Hunch together.

The twins saw their parents desperately zipping in and out of time and place, hiding bits of Roberta as they went, so that nobody would be able to seize the little robot and open the dimension door. The bright light danced with them everywhere, like Tinker Bell. Soon Roberta was only a torso and two running legs.

Mist swirled again in the crystal ball and they saw two

chubby toddlers playing with a cute black piglet, while an elephant's trunk hovered protectively overhead. Into the picture whirled the time-traveling Sloppy parents and the dancing light. They saw the toddlers look up, open-mouthed. The light morphed into the piglet, which at once hopped onto its hind feet and began to dance.

For a heart-stopping moment Nancy and Joe saw their fleeting mother reach yearningly toward their toddler selves. Then the ball went dark.

"I remember that!" Joe cried. "I remember seeing her, just for a minute! Then she was gone!"

"I don't," said Nancy enviously. She looked at the robot, sitting quietly beside Sybil Hunch. "Roberta — do you remember where they went to hide your legs?"

"Of course not," said Roberta. "By that time your talented but improvident father had hidden my brain somewhere else." She added, reflectively, "The legs can run through time, but only the whole can breach dimensions and turn the key."

"I do remember the piglet," Nancy said. "He grew up to be Genius Kelly, of course."

"Yes, he made a good choice, this Axan fellow," Sybil Hunch said. "That pig is a Berkshire, a breed that can live for twenty years — so he knew it would still be around for your eleventh birthday. When you've found your parents, you'll all have to get him back to his own dimension before the pig dies."

"He's really a good guy, and we've deserted him!" Joe said in alarm. "Hathi just left him behind with Boppo!"

Sybil Hunch tucked her crystal ball under her cloak. "Your beneficent friend Genius-Axan isn't the brightest light in the circuit, but I think he can handle Boppo for a while. Right now your foster mother is in charge, bless her big ears."

The steady lurching rhythm of the howdah began to slow down. Hathi called over her shoulder, "Get ready! We're here!" She lifted her head and trumpeted into the night, like the first chords of the *Eroica*.

Ahead, they saw a blaze of light.

Nancy peered anxiously. "What's that?"

"I have no idea," said Sybil Hunch. "Which is a very good sign."

The Regional Conference

◆ ◆ ◆ ◆ ◆

Gregory Maguire

illustrated by James Ransome

The woods began to thin. In a stand of birches they came upon a battered rolltop office desk with a DEWEY FOR PRESIDENT IN '48 sticker on it, a stenographer's pad, a Rolodex, and an old-fashioned phone — the sort with a receiver that looks like a tortured wooden daffodil from outer space. A glass jar of disgusting brown candies stood open to the air, and unfortunate insects that had passed over the mouth of the jar and died were scattered in a nubbly way, like bits of crumpled string, all over the ink-stained green paper blotter. A wooden filing cabinet, its open drawers overcrowded with files and spilling with papers, tilted against a tree.

"They're going to blame it on the secretary, I know it," said someone, leaning down behind her desk and rooting through a bottom drawer. She emerged holding a pencil, a clipboard, and a box of pushpins and wearing spectacles that were no help since they didn't quite fit on her nose. Her nose was huge. She was an elephant, like Hathi. "Yes, yes, your names?"

Hathi put up her trunk and moved it vertically against Sybil Hunch's lips, the intergalactic signal for "Shhh! Don't say a word!" In a fuller, flutey, society-lady's voice, she cooed, "Have I put on that much avoirdupois? Don't answer that. I'm Number 47, don't you know, darling."

"Number 47, Number 47 . . ." The receptionist flipped pages and huffed. "Millions spent on time-and-galaxy travel and they can't upgrade the front office? It's a scandal. It's a disgrace. And they think frequent-flier miles are a *benefit?* Think again."

In the bottom of the howdah, Roberta remained on her back, twitching with curiosity but nervous in the presence of nastiness. Joe and Nancy peered over the edge of the conveyance. Nancy suddenly recognized the receptionist. It was Plenty Sassy, another of the elephants from the Sick and Tired Circus. Since when could she talk? For that matter, since when could *Hathi* talk? All these gabbling creatures in the circus, biding their time, minding their tongues, year after year, while Joe and Nancy had felt so alone! Together, of course, but alone . . .

"I thought you already checked in, 47," said Plenty Sassy. "Or did I make my check against 46 too large? As an elephant, my eyesight isn't all that good."

"They should let you hang up your wrinkly elephant drag," drawled Hathi. "I'd complain, darling. I *would*. It doesn't do your figure any favors, for one thing. They can't treat the staff like that."

"Well, they like to keep up appearances at the front desk," said Plenty Sassy. "In case we have any unwanted visitors. Listen, you know the drill. Sling your disguise on the nearest broken tree branch, and you'd better hurry up. They've already started."

"I need to use the little alien's room first. It was a long trip," said Hathi.

"Tell me about it. Off to your left somewhere. Not

sure how convenient the conveniences will be, sweetheart, not when they can't even supply me with a laptop. I'll tell you, this whole operation is being handled by monkeybutts. Excuse my French."

Hathi tiptoed into the foliage to the left, but once she'd gotten a safe distance from the front desk, she rustled some vegetation to cause some aural camouflage and whispered to her passengers, "Elephants are notoriously shortsighted. She never recognized me from the circus."

"Where are we?" asked Sybil Hunch. "Someplace risky. And I had such a good feeling."

"Even misfortune-tellers can have an off day," hissed Hathi. "Or maybe some good will come of this, risky or not. Now, listen: I do think this might be the aliens' regional conference. I've heard Plenty Sassy mumble about it in her sleep all these years. Apparently it only happens once a decade. We might learn a great deal if we listen in."

"I'm good at watching, but I'm not as practiced at listening," said Miss Hunch.

"Eavesdropping is sneaky and morally dubious," said Nancy.

"We're in a forest," her brother reminded her. "There are no eaves."

"That's right," said Miss Hunch. "I think, as matters go, that eavesdropping might be questionable but leaves-dropping is quite all right. Shall we?"

Joe nodded. Hathi nodded. Nancy paused and scowled, but her curiosity got the better of her and she gave a thumbs-up. "I suppose we might learn something useful," she said, "even if it's only that eavesdropping isn't morally loathsome in every instance."

Hathi inched forward.

A convenient blind of evergreens screened them all from the light glowing in the clearing beyond. "Now, hush," said Hathi. "Need I say it twice? Just in case: Hush hush."

Using her supple, elegant proboscis, she prodded the

branches. With a twitch of her nasal digit, she lifted a branch, like lifting a slat in a venetian blind, so they could all see.

The yolky light took some getting used to; Joe and Nancy squinted against the brilliance. Their eyes drifted to the left and right.

The trees and bushes were draped with dreadful pelts. A scattering of wolf skins, with glassy, artificial eyes like plastic olives. A sort of squid-sheath to which a likeness of a human head had been mounted. And behold: that objectionable couture known as Leonardo Dubenski, laid crossways on a boulder because it was hard to know which end was up. To say nothing of a couple of crones, a laughable Frankenstein noggin that wouldn't scare a kindergartner, some flea-bitten vampire capes and dentures complete with overbites, a half-dozen full-body clown costumes, and the likeness of a dental technician with death in her eyes.

Little by little, Nancy and Joe felt their eyes adjust to the glare. Sybil Hunch muttered, "All those years of staring into the crystal ball . . . especially at my place, where the reception is almost nonexistent. Can you children tell me what this is?"

"It looks to me like . . . three or four dozen poached eggs?" said Nancy. "Floating in a circle in midair?"

"Not quite cooked yet?" said Joe.

It was true; the matter was only partly congealed, and ranged from a rubber-cement transparency to a gluey, translucent white. Edges of the Eggy-Things raveled, broke off, and orbited nearby like bits of suds until they gravitated slowly back and reattached.

"We can't wait any longer!" said one of the Eggy-Things. It was a little grayer in color. Distinguished, possibly bearded, if a poached egg can ever be said to be bearded. "A few of our number have yet to arrive, but we can't postpone the proceedings for them any longer. Our exhibit A has a limited shelf life. Let the regional conference come to order!"

"Plenty Sassy didn't send out the hold-the-date notices in time," muttered one of them.

"*She's* got a cushy job," sniped another. "All the hay you can eat, and then playing cozy-cozy with that Hathi, just to keep an eye on her. Once a decade Plenty Sassy has to organize a reunion and she screws it all up? *Please.*"

"I heard that!" bellowed Plenty Sassy through the woods. "My eyes might not be keen, but there's nothing wrong with my hearing!"

Sybil Hunch raised her eyebrows and poked the kids in the ribs. They all must remain *very quiet indeed.*

"No time for personal comments," said Eggy Senior. "We have a quorum. Not that we need a quorum, because I'm the boss and a very fine and naughty dictator, if I do say so myself. And whoever arrives late will have to stay after and clean up the refreshments. So ha ha and boo-boo on them. Now. First, I'd like a report from Number 17, the agent who goes as Boppo the clown." As he spoke, the yolky heart of him blurred with mouthing motions — like a sock puppet made from a room-temperature coconut custard, on the loose and floating around, looking for trouble.

"Boppo's not here. He's asleep," said someone. "I passed him on my way here."

"Why didn't you wake him up?"

"My disguise is as a poison butterfly. I didn't have the influence. Anyway, it's not my fault if Boppo drifts off to sleep at the drop of a meatball."

"Narcolepsy," said someone else witheringly.

"Narcolepsy, my foot," said another. "Hey, my foot just fell asleep. Do I have walking narcolepsy?"

They all laughed bitterly, and shook when they laughed like a bowlful of — well, never mind.

"It's my belief," said the fourth voice, "that Boppo has developed a fondness for that soporific gingerbread he makes to disarm his enemies. He tucks into it when no one is looking."

"Sassy, make a note of that," called Eggy Senior.

"I already did. With a *pencil*. Gotta love the technological revolution!" she bellowed.

"Let's hear from Number 24, then. The squid. What can you tell us?"

"If you had given us better warning about not touching the Corpse pieces when we found them, I wouldn't have a human face on the top of my cephalopod body," said another Eggy-Thing. "I almost had Sloppy Joe in my tentacles, but he tricked me into arm wrestling with him, and then he escaped along with Arm Number One. I think having a face like a retired civil servant didn't help my concentration."

"Tell me about it," said the Eggy-Thing with the voice like Leonardo Dubenski. "I forgot the little disaster that happened to me when I touched Arm Number Two, so then when out of habit I went to brush my teeth with the electric toothbrush — well, let's just say it wasn't pretty."

"How come Boppo could carry the robot's heart and its brain without suffering a curse of terrible ugliness?" asked someone else. "It hardly seems fair."

"Are you kidding? We're talking *Boppo*. He's already

disfigured enough." They shook with laughter again, coming dangerously close to scrambling themselves. Even Joe and Nancy snickered, which was something of a relief after all this tension. It *was* pretty funny. Sybil Hunch pinched them both, hard, to make them stop.

"No, really," said the Eggy-Thing who had asked the question. "Funning aside."

"Boppo has earned a kind of immunity," said Eggy Beard. "He brought our prisoner into custody. Look, we can't wait for Boppo to get here. We better bring out exhibit A."

"Bring out the prisoner!" cried the other aliens. Joe and Nancy glanced at each other. Mom? Dad? Baby Max? But they were all in another dimension, weren't they? Still, their hearts leapt up. Just in case.

"The prisoner!" chorused the Eggy-Things.

"Keep your pants on," brayed Plenty Sassy. "I only got one nose."

They heard the rustling of leaves and the snapping of twigs. The secretary elephant lumbered into the clearing carrying a kind of birdcage. Inside it, hunched and smaller than he had once been, squatted Einstein.

"I thought he was only a projection of Genius Kelly!"

Joe was merely mouthing, but Nancy telepathically — and through the movement of his lips — could tell what he meant. She shrugged. Who knew? But seeing Einstein again — loopy and dear as he'd seemed — felt like meeting up with a long-lost grandfather. That is, given the scarcity of other close relatives to cherish.

With the tiniest of beeps, Roberta made a kind of mechanical purr. She must have been recognizing Einstein, too! Sybil Hunch put a calming palm upon Roberta's headless shoulder.

"How wonderful of Boppo to have severed this aerial projection from our opposite number that they call Genius Kelly," said Eggy Senior. "This quivering hologram won't last forever, of course. Attributes rarely do. But before he fades perhaps we can learn a little something useful from him."

"Ooooooooh," said the other Eggies, nudging one another with their elbows. Sort of. If you can think of giant partly poached eggs hovering in a forest clearing as being able to give elbow.

"Time is of the essence to a three-minute egg," said the leader, at which they all chortled — apparently an old joke, but they seemed to react as if to say, Aren't the old jokes the

best? Joe and Nancy rolled their eyes at each other. This
sounded like chatter from the old-time radio era of a yolk-a-
minute comedy hour.

"Einstein, or Brainstain, or Greenbean, or whatever
you're called," continued Eggy Senior. "As a flitch of Genius
Kelly — a kind of tossed-up bright shadow of his own thinking, created through the Exquisite Corpse method for the
purpose of foiling our plans — tell us what you know about
the location of the Corpse's memory."

The Einstein apparition spoke in a voice much more
timid than when the children had first met him. Their hearts
pounded to hear him so frail. "It seems that the children
have found Roberta's heart and her mind," said Einstein, and
allowed himself a bitten-off smile. Roberta gave a mechanical
thumbs-up.

"We know that!" roared Eggy Senior, and all the other
Eggy-Things roared too. A chorus of roaring eggs is a ter-
rifying thing to behold. Also to hear. "But in her *memory* is
the knowledge of where all the remaining pieces must be. If
we can find her memory before those pesky brats do, we can
snatch the other pieces and keep Roberta from being fully
rehabilitated."

But, thought Nancy, glancing at what they had so far of Roberta, *a fully functioning Roberta is the only ally who can help us rescue our parents!*

"*I'm* not going to reach for another piece of the Exquisite Corpse," said the Eggy-Thing with the squid voice. "What'll it be next, naked human knees right in the middle of each tentacle?"

"Tell me about it," muttered the Leonardo Dubenski Eggy-Thing voice. "Ain't gonna happen. Have you heard about Number 16 and her millipede problem? She's got mustaches where she has no business shaving."

"You'll do what I tell you!" bellowed Eggy Senior. "Don't forget, you'll be richly compensated for your pains once we get home and Plenty Sassy processes the forms."

"Ha ha." From a quarter mile away, Plenty Sassy snorted without humor. "That's my first priority. Right. Processing payments. With a chalkboard and an abacus. Ha double ha."

"It's too late," said Einstein. "I know I am about to flicker out, remaining little more than a memory to any who might care to remember me. But I will tell you this, you monstrous aliens without the benefit of hearts, shells, or the decency to wrap yourselves in a velvety hollandaise. Roberta already *has* her memory. The truth is that memory isn't something extractable, like a tooth, or a spleen. Memory is the sum of what is generated between the heart and the mind. It's the Exquisite Corpse of a human life. That's it."

"*Ooo-oooh,*" said the Eggy-Things. They had never thought of this.

"And furthermore," said Einstein, "while I'm on the subject, E=mc²? Energy equals mass times the speed of light squared? *Not!* I left out the secret ingredient! All good cooks do it. Preserves the mystery, and also their reputations." He began to shimmer in the air before them and to fade, but as he disappeared he raised his voice as if to address the planet. "I loved you, Baby Max! Thank you, dear Genius Kelly, for carrying me in your memory! Remember, if anyone useful should be listening in the ferns or in the future, that the missing ingredient is found in the joke book! Which is in the drawer with the *eggbeater!* My candle's snuffed at both ends; it did not last the night. But ah, my foes and likewise friends, the light! The light! Good-bye!"

And out he went, like a candle. No blue radiating glow where he'd been this time. Just emptiness.

The Eggy-Things began to mutter among themselves.

They looked like a giant floating baked Alaska, except lit with the light of their inner badness. Plenty Sassy lurched forward, pushing a trolley with her trunk, but Sybil Hunch guessed that the Eggy-Things would need to dress in their corporeal disguises to be able to help themselves to tea and some vile little cookies. Sybil Hunch tickled Hathi behind her right ear and made a motion with her head as if to say, *Outta here, sister.*

While they snack, thought Nancy, *could we steal a lead?* Although stealing is generally considered unsavory, morally speaking.

Hathi backed up delicately, stealthily. For the first time in quite a while, the Sloppy kids heard no sinister voice mocking or cursing or threatening them from the next chapter. Just the silence — it trembled strangely in the tree limbs with its own particular gravity — of the evaporation of something that had resembled a human soul. They didn't speak. Every death — the death of hope, of fondness, of an enemy or a friend, even the death of an apparition — deserves a little respectful silence.

LEGS ON THE RUN

✦ ✦ ✦ ✦

SHANNON HALE

illustrated by CALEF BROWN

They continued out of the forest, the only sounds the creak of the howdah on Hathi's back, the soft thuds of the elephant's feet on the ground, and Joe's calls of "a little to the right, Hathi" and "straight ahead" as he consulted the red arrow on his toe. Roberta was motionless, as if in rest mode. There were blankets in the howdah, and Nancy snuggled in, warm between Sybil and Joe. She let her mind go soft and slept some.

When the east began to wake with light, so did her mind, but she kept her eyes shut and thought. Boppo hadn't seemed like much, what with his fascination with gobs of spiced meat and tendency to nap on the go, but he'd found Roberta's heart and brain before she and Joe could. And as soon as the regional conference and snack time was over, that pack of eggy monsters they'd left in the forest would robe themselves again in their guises of villains, cads, and scalawags and be on the hunt.

"We have to find Roberta's legs before they do," Joe said, sensing her thoughts.

"And maybe her head, too?" said Nancy. "I'm confused: if she already has her brain, does she need a head?"

"Those yolk-ers back there said that Roberta's memory should know the legs' location."

"But Roberta's brain was removed before they were hidden," said Sybil, yawning like a tiger.

"That is most accurate," Roberta said in a crisp British accent. Her boxy torso sat on the floor of the howdah, the arms crossed, and she looked as exquisitely dignified as a metal box with arms can.

"But . . . but you did say something about the legs. . . ." Joe scrunched up his nose, trying to remember. "You said they can run through time."

No one replied. Hathi had just entered a village.

The elephant paraded past bungalow homes with front porches, parks with swings nudged by a breeze, but not a person in sight. The arrows pointed them in toward the village center, mom-and-pop stores surrounding a grassy square where a massive chestnut tree held court.

"What happened here?" said Joe. "It's so empty."

"And familiar . . ." It took Nancy a moment to recall: she'd seen that chestnut tree in Sybil's crystal ball, her parents beneath it, handing their babies over to Ringmaster.

"An elephant never forgets." Hathi lifted her trunk and breathed in deeply. "The Sick and Tired Circus raised its big top here ten years ago."

There was a dark shape under the tree, whuffling around. Nancy clutched the scar on her left arm, afraid it was the wolf, until the shape lifted its head and oinked.

"Genius Kelly!" said Joe.

A sudden pain flashed in Nancy's left arm, and her head was awash with images — something coming, coming quickly, coming toward them. . . .

"Go!" said Nancy.

Without question, Hathi went faster, running like an

earthquake toward the pig and the tree. Joe gripped the edge of the box and stared back to see which terror was chasing them now.

Around the corner, passing the abandoned hardware store, came the wolf. In its speed, it was all sleek silver fur and teeth, and it looked exactly like the very last thing you'd want coming straight for you. The wolf's teeth were gritty black, stained with the supermarket-brand cookies Plenty Sassy had served (Good Time Bites: 23% wax, 77% fun!). But even if Joe had known the dark grit was simply cookie crumbs and not the grimy blood of helpless victims (as he naturally supposed), it still wouldn't have softened the impression of a dastardly, interdimensional demon with death on its mind.

Hathi had reached the chestnut tree, and an elephant knows when she's been outrun. She turned to face the predator, standing between wolf and pig, her trunk raised.

It's going to leap, Nancy thought — no, *knew. It's going to leap, knock me out of the way, grab Roberta in its mouth, and gnaw her to bits, and my parents will be trapped forever. I have to stop him. But I can't. I can't. . . .*

"Nancy!" Joe yelled. "Lollipop!"

Nancy felt at her waist — she still had it! The knife

she'd been carrying in her belt since Baby Max picked it off one of Dubenski's thieves. No, babies should not play with knives . . . but Nancy thought *thank you* all the same.

The wolf leapt for the howdah, claws and teeth first. Nancy aimed the dagger, trying to imagine that the creature's throat was just a circus balloon, like the ones she used to pop from a distance for the amazed crowd. She threw it. Bull's-eye. Or rather, wolf's-throat.

No clapping crowd now, just the wolf's howl, a sound like time itself ripping. It dropped to the ground and clawed at the knife in its pelt.

"You can never defeat us," said Nancy, shaking hands placed firmly on her hips. "Interdimensional badness always loses in the end, and you just lost."

"Yeah," said Joe.

"Perhaps I did," the wolf said, its eyes beginning to look like glass, its jaw starting to hang slack. "But I am not alone."

The rend in the wolf's throat opened wider, screaming like a zipper. The eggy being inside slurped and slid out and rose up, just out of reach of Hathi's seven-foot trunk. Lurid yellow light began to pulse from its center, like a beacon of ovular horror.

Hathi trumpeted at it. "Stop that, you repulsive roe!"

"I don't need to consult the ball to see that's no good," said Sybil.

Nancy leapt from Hathi's back and dropped beside Genius Kelly, who was hiding behind one of Hathi's great pillar legs and staring at the egg in the sky.

"How did you come here?" Nancy asked.

"I followed my arrow to this spot, but . . . it's empty," he whimper-oinked.

Nancy removed her sock and walked around, and sure enough her toe arrow pointed forward, then as she passed over an ordinary spot on the grass, the arrow swung around and pointed backward again.

Joe was gathering chestnuts for Hathi to shoot with her trunk at the globby alien. The chestnuts struck and entered the slurpy mass but didn't affect its eerie pulsing light.

"That's one nutty omelet," Joe breathed. He didn't know what the alien was doing up there, but fear pricked every goose bump on his skin.

"Joe, we need you!" Nancy called.

She explained her plan. The three arrowed ones stood several feet from one another in a rough circle, then began to walk forward, following the direction of their own toe arrows, working to triangulate the exact location. Joe considered that if he actually used the word *triangulate* out loud, he'd never get invited to parties, but he went along with the plan anyway.

"There!" said Nancy when she was standing shoulder to shoulder with Joe and Genius. "All our arrows are pointing to that spot. Something should be right here."

She swished her hand around, wondering if there was a piece of the Exquisite Corpse hovering invisible before her, but she felt nothing. "Could it be buried?"

"Then our arrows would point down," said Joe. They were amazingly accurate little arrows.

Roberta darted through Joe's legs and hopped about on her hands, speaking impatiently. "Here, something is here! Or near. Nearly here . . ."

"Joe, remember what Roberta said earlier about the legs?"

Joe met eyes with his sister and nodded. "The legs could be in this spot, but running through time, so if we wait here —"

"They'll come our way again."

Sybil was hunched over her crystal ball. Her hood fell back, exposing a head of white frizz as crazy as a clown's wig. "I might have been a cobbler, or a fine purveyor of persimmon punch," she mumbled. "Instead I have the misfortune of foretelling our coming doom."

Genius Kelly's head whipped toward Sybil, his snout quivering.

"Doom?" It was Genius Kelly's least favorite word, followed closely by *loin chop*.

Sybil didn't need to explain. They could all see the motion in her ball — the clawing, snapping, galloping mass of creatures leaping over each other to arrive first.

"They're coming," said Joe. "For us. Egg Man up there is broadcasting our position, I'd bet the tattooed lady's serpentined limbs."

"Maybe we'll have Roberta's legs before the rabble arrives," Nancy said, dredging up some of that Sloppy pluck.

"Keep a keen eye, children," said Hathi. She winked her small, gray one and pointed her trunk to the spot they surrounded.

Nancy grabbed Joe's hand. It was hot and sweaty. Or was that her own? Roberta lifted up one of her arms and Nancy reached out, but pulled it back as soon as her fingers touched the half-formed robot. Something had felt wrong, the way it feels when the dentist deadens your gums and you

probe those numb places with your tongue. Nancy looked at
the thin white scar the wolf had left on her arm and shuddered. It *was* changing her. Her Sloppy DNA should make
her immune to the dangerous mechanisms protecting every
part of Roberta. So what *had* happened when the wolf cut
her? Had there been poison on his claws? Did part of his
eggy mass get inside her wound and begin to change her very
DNA? Was she . . . *oh, no* . . . was she becoming one of *them?*

"Joe, you hold Roberta's hand," Nancy said, trying to
sound calm.

"Right," said Joe. "And we'll grab those legs as soon
as they appear, which will be long before the arrival of the
squids with human heads, maniacal clowns, werewolves,
and those other things we saw at their conference — poison
butterflies, vampires, dental technicians —"

"Don't think about it," said Nancy. "Think about the
house we'll live in with Mom and Dad when this is all over."

A house. A real house, not a tent or boxcar. Maybe
Nancy could have a bed — her first. In her mind, the essen-
tial purpose of a bed was to provide a place where one might
be Tucked In, and at that moment, bracing against the arrival
of foes known and new, being Tucked In sounded like the
most glorious event in all the world.

Joe fantasized about a couch. He'd read about couches and caught glimpses of them through windows whenever the Sick and Tired Circus passed through towns. The circus had chairs and stools, but they are furniture of solitude. There were benches, too, which are more social, but the hard seat and lack of back says, "Rest for a moment if you must, then move along." But a couch says, "Here, take a load off, sit close and comfy with some family, and stay as long as you like." A couch is where a boy can plop down to read a book with a mother. A couch is the foundation of a good fort, where a boy and his father can hide beneath blankets and plan infiltrations of the kitchen.

"Bed," Nancy said dreamily.

"Couch," Joe said wistfully.

"Doom," Genius Kelly said emphatically.

And around the corner from the hardware store, howls, snarls, yips, and whoops chorused.

Nancy's dagger was still stuck in the fake wolf skin on the grass, where it had sloughed off the now-pulsing Egg Man.

"It's too late," she said, going for the knife. "The legs didn't appear. We need to fight now."

"No, wait," said Hathi.

"Wait," Sybil agreed. "We'll buy you time." She stood up, stowed her ball in her robe, and brushed off her hands. "Your parents knew — most problems are solved by time."

Genius Kelly whimpered. He looked at the two ladies — one gray-haired, one gray-skinned — then sighed. "Yes, wait for the legs. We'll hold off the rabble."

Hathi broke a wooden park bench with one crunch of her foreleg and hoisted a lethal-looking piece in her trunk. She turned toward the oncoming enemy. Sybil was at her side. When her hands twitched, vines peeked up out of the ground and tensed forward, like hounds awaiting their master's call. Genius Kelly wobbled up between them, set his front hoof, and growled.

"We can't let them fight alone," said Nancy.

"Watch," Roberta warned. "Watch with all vigilance. Watch." She gave a long, piercing whine of a beep, as if in her alarm, she reverted briefly to her voiceless, brainless self.

Nancy took Joe's hand again. The air between them was suddenly colder, and yet it wobbled like the heat haze over a summer street.

Joe stared at that air, stared at it violently, refusing to look behind him, though every cell in his body was aware of the trumpeting and screaming, snarls and slaps, yelps and snorgles, and one very distinct oink. There was a sharp cry like a hurt elephant and Joe almost broke, but though his lower lip quivered just a little, he kept his gaze on that empty spot of grass.

Then with no more warning, two metallic legs shivered into view, one slightly forward, one back, as if they were indeed running.

"Now!" shouted Nancy, the legs already flickering out.

Nancy, Joe, and Roberta leapt forward, pouncing on the legs. Their momentum should have pulled them forward, the three of them pinning the legs to the grass. But instead came the unexpected, stomach-squeezing, throat-clamping, scream-inducing tug to the side, as if what they'd grabbed was a roller-coaster car zipping at high speed. It was wrong and it was scary and it didn't stop. The world was a mangled blur of colors and darkness; the noise was like being locked in a dryer on high.

Nancy screamed. Her scream went on and on, dragging out of her even after she was certain her mouth was shut and her breath held. Her scarred arm couldn't bear to touch those legs, but she squeezed Joe's hand tight as if it were a buoy in a tossing sea.

Finally, the ground found them with a thud. Joe

groaned, a metal knee in his gut. He still held Roberta's hand with his right and Nancy's with his left, and they appeared to be in the same place as before: the village center under the tall chestnut tree, empty buildings staring back. But the light was different — no longer morning, but high noon. The air was as chilly as the dairy aisle, and most importantly, Sybil, Genius Kelly, and Hathi, as well as the mob of danger-cloaked eggy villains, were gone.

Roberta stood up — yes, stood. A no-nonsense android who has been missing her legs for ten years won't waste time snapping them back on. She put her hands on her hip region and squared her shoulder-type area toward Joe and Nancy, as if meeting them with the steely gaze she surely would have if she'd had a head.

"I should think, *mes enfants,* that now is the time to find a door."

An Angel Descends

✦ ✦ ✦ ✦

Steven Kellogg

illustrated by Timothy Basil Ering

Now that Joe and Nancy and the robot had actually disappeared and the aliens were fast approaching, Genius Kelly felt his determination to defend his beloved friends was muddled by creeping feelings of insecurity, doubt, and dread. To bolster his courage, he looked closely at his two allies. Hathi was certainly large and stalwart. He watched her swing the fragment of park bench that she had snatched up to use as a weapon, and her intensity made him glad that they were on the same side. She had mothered Joe and Nancy during their years in the circus, and looking at her expression of maternal commitment assured him that she would be a formidable foe against any evil creature who tried to fight its way past her in order to do them harm.

As for Sybil Hunch, the misfortune-teller seemed to have some minor talents as a magician, but Genius Kelly doubted that she would be particularly impressive as a warrior. She had not known the twins very long, but she had developed a grandmotherly feeling of tenderness for them, and he had been impressed when she forthrightly volunteered to help hold off the aliens while they took Roberta and made good their escape.

Genius Kelly's review of his forces buoyed his spirits. "Things could be worse," he said to himself. "One of the troops is bulky and tough, and the other one is wiry and courageous." He plucked up his own courage, remembering that he had been charged with being the children's protector. And, even though he was a circus dancer and not a soldier, he had another talent that he thought might surprise the aliens in the event that hand-to-hand combat was called for!

Genius Kelly suggested to Hathi and Sybil Hunch that they decide on a strategy before the aliens arrive. "Although we have absolutely no chance of winning," he said, "we have the advantage of being united by the high purposes of loyalty and self-sacrifice! Above all, we must remember that we achieve an important victory, no matter how dismally things turn out for us, by gaining time for our friends to complete their mission. Joe and Nancy's success depends on us! We will not let them down! ONWARD!" The brave trio exchanged hugs of encouragement and solidarity, and then turned to await the appearance of the enemy.

For their assault, the aliens had assumed dark and menacing shapes, and their eyes had been carefully calibrated to blaze and flash like neon lights. Suddenly the order to attack was zapped into them from their command post. Sneering and snarling, they charged from the shadows and flung themselves at their adversaries. The first one to reach Genius Kelly was not prepared for the pig's professional cool as he expertly blocked the first blow and then whirled gracefully and flipped his assailant head over heels. This was the talent that the dancing pig had thought might surprise his adversaries! Joe and Nancy had known of Genius Kelly's familiarity with judo because when they had expressed an interest in the martial arts, he had given them lessons. Now, however, his enthusiasm for the sport was put to serious use as he grappled with a succession of alien opponents and briskly sent each of them sprawling.

Sybil Hunch had meanwhile used her magic powers to recruit a troupe of compliant ivy vines exactly as she had done at another critical moment earlier in the adventure. This time she directed the vines to coordinate their movements, binding up each fallen alien as tightly, neatly, and helplessly as hapless beetles are packaged in spider webbing.

As for Hathi, she wielded the fragment of park bench with the dexterity of a tennis pro. Thinking of her beloved Joe and Nancy in danger aroused her to an astonishing level of martial efficiency. She whacked first one alien and then backhanded another, shoving each of them into the clutches of the vines where they were quickly put out of action.

It seemed that the victory that had been inconceivable was now actually at hand! Sybil Hunch dodged and skipped through the turmoil, deploying her cadre of vines with the shrewd military instincts of Napoleon. She made certain that every alien that was toppled by Genius Kelly or bashed by Hathi was ensnarled by her vines before it could recover. Soon very few of them were left standing.

But then a wave of alien reinforcements poured in. They were protected by helmets and riot gear, and they were armed with electronic pitchforks, lances, and cattle prods that permitted them to poke, sting, and bruise the Sloppy twins' defenders, and to drive them in any desired direction. The valiant trio lost momentum and stumbled in confusion, as the aliens gleefully taunted them and herded them toward a strange structure. It turned out to be the boxing ring that had been moved from the clearing where it had been utilized by Baby Max as a roller-skating rink during happier times. Now it served as a command post for the aliens' leader, a huge, hulking, cloaked and masked figure who was feverishly transmitting signals from his official Military Palm Pilot/Puppeteer #CJX7382. As ordered, the alien troops drove Genius Kelly, Hathi, and Sybil Hunch back against the command post and pinned them there. Above them the leader wheeled around and threw off his cloak, revealing a grotesque gorilla body that was covered by densely tangled tattoos. When he moved, they wriggled and rolled over muscles that bulged like bloated watermelons. The combatants on both sides froze when he roared, "SILENCE!" He ripped off his mask, exposing a ghastly head transplant. It was none other than the hideous, blank, rear-end face of Leonardo Dubenski! A teleprompter popped from beneath the canvas, and he launched into a speech, bellowing, "I am the Villain of Villains, and the Toughest Hunk of Scum in the Underworld! Invaders, this is your Day of Doom!" He paused to glare down at his victims. (That is, they assumed he was glaring. It is difficult to read the expressions on a face that is, in actuality, a rear end.)

"On the plus side," whispered Genius Kelly to Sybil Hunch, "it looks like this will be a long-winded speech, which will give Joe and Nancy more time to escape."

"On the minus side, and speaking of wind," she whispered back, "his breath STINKS!"

"Shhhh! Be quiet! Shut up!" hissed a number of the aliens, poking their weapons threateningly in the direction of their prisoners, who instantly fell silent.

Dubenski's face swelled as he took a deep breath and continued in an even louder voice: "Now, to avenge the humiliation of the squid by the fugitive punk you have been protecting, I challenge you —"

But the challenge was cut short by Hathi, who, propelled by a surge of blind motherly outrage, bounded into the ring, trumpeting hysterically, "My Joe is no punk! BEWARE! You insult him at your peril! My ancestors marched with Hannibal and squashed the Romans!"

Dubenski was so startled by her outburst that he lost track of the line he had been reading. Before he could find his place, Hathi reared up and smacked him with her bench fragment so smartly that his head-butt was driven like a squarely struck nail directly down into his body and out of sight. The headless, tatooed torso, with arms flailing, staggered in circles like a drunken dancer. Then he blundered into the ropes and bounced over backward onto the canvas, emitting a disgusting, volcanic belch. Hathi's teammates applauded and cheered, "HATHI! HATHI! HATHI!" as she stepped triumphantly from the ring, while the aliens gaped in disbelief. They were clearly stunned by the spectacle of the previously undefeated Dubenski being hustled off to the underworld locker room even before he had delivered his carefully composed challenge!

It only took a moment, however, for the villains to rally and to change their tactics. Hissing, "VENGEANCE! VENGEANCE! VENGEANCE!" the ones that had been wrapped in vines oozed from between their bonds, while the others, steaming with fury, began to disintegrate into gelatinous, eggy blobs. To the horror of Hathi, Genius Kelly, and Sybil Hunch, the blobs flowed together, increasing in size and mounding themselves around the trio like a vile, pulsating meringue . . . like a living swamp . . . like a monstrous, murderous amoeba! As the glob rose above their feet, gluing them into place, Sybil Hunch chanted frantic imprecations summoning magical forces that did not respond. Genius Kelly wailed and thrashed helplessly. And Hathi trumpeted to the skies like one of her tragic pre-Hannibal, mastodon ancestors mired in the deadly muck of the La Brea Tar Pits.

But, just as the goo was swelling exultantly and rising to engulf its victims' knees, torsos, and heads, the skies lit up and a voice from above called cheerfully, "Hello, Jell-O! Angel's here! Release my friends, and DISAPPEAR!"

Nancy and Joe had told Genius Kelly all about this helpful pirate named Angel who had seemed to possess information about their mission when they had met up with him earlier in their adventure. "Hallelujah! Welcome, Angel!" cried the pig.

The pirate addressed the threatening substance with more authority. "I repeat, Blob," he hollered. "LEAVE AT ONCE!"

The mound instantly ceased to swell. For a moment every ripple was paralyzed, and then the entire mass began

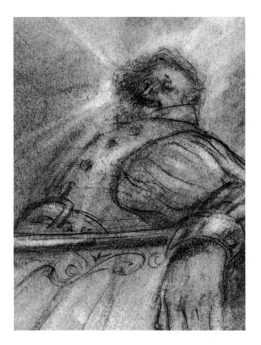

to sag like a deflating balloon. Finally the pool of goo fragmented, and then reshaped itself into individual egg yolks.

"GO!" commanded Angel with a grand, dismissive gesture.

The chastised yolks slithered back into the shadows, but their renewed, whispered threats of "vengeance, vengeance, vengeance" promised trouble ahead.

For the moment, however, all was joy and peace. The three rescued adventurers gazed in wonder at Angel, who beamed benevolently down at them. He looked resplendent as he descended in an impressive craft that was instantly recognizable as the monumental and magical Cradle of Time.

"I'm here to evacuate you pooped-out pilgrims," he announced. He vaulted to the ground, and lifted each of them into the cradle.

Watching the pirate, who was as strong and agile as a gymnast, hoisting the elephant without any apparent effort made Genius Kelly wish that Angel had arrived a bit earlier, when they were being bullied by Dubenski.

"Don't you worry," said Angel, uncannily reading the pig's thoughts. "I wouldn't let that thug turn you into bacon! I was about to erase his tattoos, but Ms. Hathi nailed him first. She is one powerful pachyderm! Don't mess with her!"

There was no response from the exhausted elephant, who was sleeping blissfully in a corner of the cradle. Sybil Hunch was curled beside her.

"I pushed the naptime button on the cradle's panel," confided Angel to Genius Kelly. The pig responded with drooping eyes and a drowsy nod.

"Time to sag, Protector," Angel said with a chuckle. "You're off duty." He lifted the pig and gently placed him beside his companions. Then he covered the sleeping trio with a fluffy quilt.

After punching more entries into the panel, Angel tilted the cradle slightly, and the years suddenly fell away from its three occupants. Genius Kelly became a piglet, Hathi reverted to an elephant calf, and Sybil Hunch was once again a wiry, frizzy-haired kindergartner.

"Sweet dreams, babies. You're back in time, before worries and troubles make life tough. You'll sleep much better back there," murmured Angel. Then he added wistfully, "I wish the twins were with us now. They'd think they were almost home." He sighed, pushed the set button on the panel, and leapt nimbly into the cradle.

The Cradle of Time rose like a grand gondola drawn upward by an invisible balloon. It sailed serenely through the radiant sunshine and the canyons of clouds. Meanwhile the napping friends, exhausted from all the stress generated by their confrontation with the aliens, enjoyed the sweet dreams that Angel had wished for them.

After several hours, the three sleepers began to stir.

"Time to grow up now, youngsters," said Angel. He reprogrammed and retilted the cradle to bring them back to their former maturity levels. It took a few moments for their interior biological systems to adjust to the jolts and swellings brought about by the abrupt change in age, but a few burps, hiccoughs, and sneezes later, everything was functioning harmoniously.

They felt blissfully rested after their nap, but decidedly HUNGRY! The ever-thoughtful and resourceful Angel had anticipated this possibility. He winked at the computer panel, and like magic, three gloved hands emerged from a trapdoor and delivered a delicious-looking trio of trays. Each of the platters was heaped with gourmet fare that was perfectly chosen to delight the palate of a pig, an elephant, and a misfortune-teller. With mouths full and cheeks bulging, the three friends heaped praise and gratitude on their beaming host, labeling him "a prince, a saint, a champion, and a hero," as well as an angel.

When second helpings of dessert had been devoured, Angel asked, "What's the next move, folks?"

"Heavens! We've got to find Nancy and Joe!" declared Genius Kelly, suddenly jolted back to reality and remembering who it was he had been charged to protect.

"We're in Nancy and Joe's time frame now," said Angel reassuringly. He had already locked the cradle into the proper time slot to coincide with the band in which the twins and Roberta were operating. And, sure enough, there they were in the distance. As the cradle swept downward, Angel programmed the sound-search system to pick up their conversation. Roberta was completing a sentence that ended with the intriguing observation "Now is the time to find a door."

ANYTHING AT ALL

✦ ✦ ✦ ✦

LINDA SUE PARK

illustrated by CHRIS VAN DUSEN

The reunion was a joyful one, relief on all sides spilling over into elation.

"How did you find us so fast?" Joe exclaimed.

Raised eyebrows from Angel and Sybil; Genius Kelly would have raised his eyebrows, too, if he'd had any. He settled for a snort instead.

"Wasn't all that fast," Angel said. "I picked up the gang a while back, and we've been on the lookout for you ever since."

"You mean, *you* were on the lookout," Hathi pointed out. "Credit where credit is due, dear. The rest of us were asleep."

Nancy shook her head. "It must have been the time frame we were in," she said. "We only just got Roberta's legs attached and were trying to figure out what to do next when Joe spotted the cradle."

"That is not entirely accurate," Roberta said. "We *know* what to do next: we need to find that door." She stretched out her newly attached legs in front of her and looked fondly at her articulated knees.

"Roberta, you got legs!" Angel said, grinning. "They're lookin' mighty fine, lady."

"Why, thank you, Angel," Roberta replied, crossing her ankles with a loud clank. "I must say, I am pleased to have them back. I rather missed them."

She paused, and when she spoke again, her voice was quieter. "I'm feeling a great deal better now, but I do wonder if we'll ever find my head. I must confess that I don't feel quite myself without it."

"Of course we'll find it!" Nancy said stoutly, and patted the robot on the shoulder. Nancy thought that it must be awful for Roberta, not having a head. Even if a human being could live without one, who would want to?

Besides, finding Roberta's head would mean the completion of the Exquisite Corpse — the only chance she and Joe had of finding their parents.

"I don't wish to alarm anyone," Roberta said, "but I have a feeling it needs to be soon. I am currently operating by rerouting certain functions as necessary, which is putting quite a strain on my circuitry. If my hard drive should blow — well, finding my head after that wouldn't be of any help, I'm afraid."

Silence, as the group took in what the robot had said.

Sybil shifted her position a little. Joe sniffed at the air and his mouth began watering. What was that smell? It seemed to be coming from Sybil's direction. . . .

"*Chocolate?*"

He stared at Sybil's chin, which displayed evidence of a serious and recent encounter with, at the very least, a chocolate-like substance.

"Wh-where did you get chocolate?" Nancy asked, swallowing hard. She realized that tension had been the only thing filling her stomach. When was the last time they'd eaten?

Sybil stuck out her tongue and licked her chin. "Not, strictly speaking, chocolate," she said. "It was the fudge part of a hot-fudge sundae made with cookie-dough ice cream."

"AARGH!" Joe yelled, grabbing his gut in agony.

Hathi and Angel exchanged glances. "These kids need feedin'," Angel said. "They won't be any use if they don't get their strength up. What'll it be, darlin's? Whatever you want."

Nancy and Joe sat with their mouths agape. It was Joe who found his voice first.

"Whatever we want?" he croaked. "You mean — you mean, like, anything? Is this some kind of joke?" Because if it was, he didn't think it was very funny.

Angel shrugged. "Well, I couldn't rightly say," he said. "Could be there's somethin' that won't come out of this here machine" — he tapped the computer panel of the cradle — "but if there is, nobody's asked for it yet."

Sybil began ticking off on her fingers. "I had two donuts: one glazed, one with sprinkles; a double-shot espresso with cinnamon foam; a bag of caramels; and a piece of lemon-meringue pie," she said. "And the sundae."

Nancy's awe was overcome by momentary concern. "That's an awful lot of sugar," she said.

Sybil shrugged. "Always did have a sweet tooth."

"Peanuts," Hathi said. "Unsalted, shell on. And eleven pounds of a delectable alfalfa-clover hay mix."

"I had me a shrimp gumbo," Angel said. "The real deal. Okra, and filé powder, and a roux near dark as me. Mmm-mm."

Genius Kelly opened his mouth to speak, but Joe cut him off. He didn't think he could bear listening to a list of what the pig had ordered and eaten. "What are you going to have, Nancy?" Joe asked, his eyes wide with eagerness.

He still couldn't quite believe it. Those very rare times when grown-ups said, "You can have whatever you want," what they really meant was, "You can have anything on the menu" or "You can have any candy bar in the display."

But *anything* at all? Really and truly?

Nancy's stomach grumbled and growled; any minute now, it would start barking. She needed something warm . . . soothing . . . nourishing. . . .

"Oatmeal," she blurted out.

"*Oatmeal?*" Joe yelped in disbelief.

Nancy ignored him. "A bowl of oatmeal. *Not* instant. Homemade, and no lumps, please. With brown sugar and raisins, and some really thick cream poured on top. The kind that looks almost yellow."

"*Pizza!*" Joe shouted. "Half cheese, half pepperoni!"

"Order up," Angel said, mere moments later.

Both the oatmeal and the pizza were, of course, the best that had ever been made in the history of the universe. The replicator even managed to produce a canister of pressurized air to clean out Roberta's circuitry; she let out both a sigh and a long beep of sheer delight when Angel blasted a stream of nice fresh canned air at her innards.

Sybil looked thoughtful. "We asked that computer for other things, like binoculars," she said. "It wouldn't make them. I wonder why it came up with the canned air."

"I think I figured that one out," Genius Kelly said. "I'm guessing it only does food, and the canned air is like food to her. You might say it keeps her running well." He pointed a hoof at Roberta's legs and chortled. Everyone else groaned and rolled their eyes — except for Roberta, of course, who emitted a sound like a raspberry.

At Hathi's suggestion, Roberta shut down for a while to give her circuits a rest. After the oatmeal, Nancy had carrot and celery sticks with ranch dressing, then chocolate-dipped strawberries and two chocolate-chip cookies with a tall glass of cold milk. Joe followed his pizza with a double order of fries and a chocolate milk shake.

"Joe," Nancy admonished, "vitamins. You need to eat vegetables. Or at least some fruit."

Joe rolled his eyes, slurped his milk shake, and burped. But he was feeling so good now that he decided to oblige her. "A banana, please," he said to Angel.

Nancy looked surprised and pleased at her brother's acquiescence, but her expression changed rapidly when, after peeling the banana, he smushed two-thirds of it into his mouth at once. "Ugh — that's disgusting!" she said.

It took a while for Joe to work the banana from his cheeks down into his gullet. At last he swallowed and looked at her innocently. "Nancy, I don't get you. If I don't eat fruit, you complain; if I *do* eat fruit, you still complain! Make up your mind, would ya?"

Nancy couldn't help laughing, and the others joined in. As their laughter died down, a little wave of sadness lapped at the contentment Nancy was feeling.

It wasn't long ago that this would have seemed perfect to her. Good food, good friends, laughter. . . . But now she knew what was missing.

How could you miss something you've never really had? Neither she nor Joe had ever truly known their parents. Had she always missed them, ever since she was a baby, and just not known it? Was it *them* she was missing, or the idea of having parents? What if, when they were all reunited again, they didn't get along? Worse yet, what if it never happened — if she and Joe couldn't manage to rescue them?

Nancy felt a gentle whoosh of warm air that smelled of hay. Hathi was reaching out with her trunk to stroke Nancy's hair.

Dear, wise Hathi, who always seemed to know how Nancy was feeling. . . . Nancy leaned her cheek against Hathi's trunk.

"Are you ready, little one?" Hathi asked quietly.

The food and rest had revived and restored Nancy, and

she could see that they were having the same effect on Joe. She sat up straight and smiled at Hathi.

"A head and a door," Nancy said. "Let's do it — I'm ready."

"Me, too," Joe said. He turned to Angel. "Except, could I get a bag of sour gummy bears — to go, please?"

MEANWHILE, NEAR A MEADOW

♦ ♦ ♦ ♦ ♦

LEMONY SNICKET

illustrated by JAMES RANSOME

It is one of the sad truths of the world that while some people are enjoying sour gummy bears, others might be in circumstances less delicious, such as finding themselves trapped at the bottom of a well with their clothes all muddied, or pursued by hounds across the estate of a mad duchess, or finding out that their parents had raised them only for their long, silken hair, and now that it had grown long enough to be made into a blanket they would surely be slaughtered, or even sitting in a small tin shack listening to the cawing of ravens and the distant chatter of relieved train passengers.

This last activity was Pirandello's.

Pirandello was a young man prone to melancholy, probably due to his occupation, which kept him far from anyplace where sour gummy bears could be found. He was in charge of railway safety in a remote location bordered by woods and mountains, which he had thought would be a very exciting job, involving danger and adventure. Instead, not a single train passing through Pirandello's region had experienced even the smallest accident. No rabid ravens had leapt through the train's window to bite and infect an innocent group of monks traveling through the area. Not one inch of track had been washed out in a hailstorm, leading to the evacuation of frightened flight attendants on their day off. And not a single lock on a single door of a single cargo car had broken, causing the contents to spill out over the countryside. Pirandello had many fantasies of what might spill out during such an accident — cuckoo clocks, perhaps, chirping their way down the steep embankment, or a shipment of abandoned rollercoaster parts that Pirandello might have fashioned into a go-cart, allowing him to whoosh his way through his surroundings. And, of course, Pirandello dreamed of delicious foodstuffs that might topple out of a railway accident. Working out in the boondocks meant he was limited to

eating nuts, berries, and the occasional fish he could lure out of a nearby brook, and Pirandello would have appreciated something that couldn't be found in the wild, such as sour gummy bears, a phrase which here means "sugar and chemicals shaped vaguely like bears." But it seemed that the world's sour gummy bears were being devoured by people far away from him — total strangers, whom he might never meet.

Thus, last night's train accident was good news for Pirandello.

It was still not very clear to Pirandello the cause of the

accident. He had been sleeping in the small tin shack's large lumpy cot when the sound of squealing brakes, followed by screaming, followed by a muted explosion, woke him up. By the time he'd put his railway safety bathrobe on over his pajamas, the forest was full of passengers from the stopped train climbing down a makeshift ladder and fleeing the scene of the accident. Some of them were frightened. Some of them were angry. And some of them felt nothing but weary resignation, a phrase which here means "the sense that they were only minor characters in some large, confusing story in which the heroes were far away stuffing themselves with sweets." Pirandello managed to talk to a few of the passengers but could not quite understand what had happened. They mentioned two children. They mentioned a bomb. They mentioned a clown. But as they were not the heroes of this story, the passengers were unable to recount what exactly had occurred on board the train, and were as baffled and disappointed as Pirandello himself, stumbling around the woods with his official, dimming flashlight.

If any readers are similarly confused, they might reread the first chapter of this story.

As it was so late at night and such a remote location,

most of the passengers took shelter in the woods, and when he returned to his shack Pirandello could see the distant lights of campfires and could hear the passengers talking to one another and sharing refreshments. The refreshments were likely delicious, and far more interesting than Pirandello's usual scavenged diet, but no one thought to offer anything to the melancholy man in charge of railway safety. Soon Pirandello heard the tuning of a guitar, and then a passenger began to sing, and then another, and soon a whole group, and before long the forest was full of the sounds of singing. It was a happy song, but still the chorus in the night made Pirandello feel even more melancholy than ever.

The song was "The Surrey with the Fringe On Top," which he had never liked.

Finally the passengers quieted, and before long the air was filled with the sound of ravens welcoming the dawn, and Pirandello sighed and listened to the passengers packing their things for the long hike back to where they lived. After so long, finally something interesting had happened to him, and yet he felt thwarted, a word which here means "as if he had missed his opportunity to do or find something crucial to the story."

A knock on the tin door brought him out of his thoughts. "Yes?" he called.

"Are you the person in charge of railway safety?" asked a bright voice.

"Yes," Pirandello said, and opened the door. There stood a tall, strong-looking girl with hair so short she was practically bald.

"Thank goodness," she said. "There's something I need you to see."

"Pirandello, at your service," he replied, which is something he'd always wanted to say.

"My name is Orlando," said the tall girl. "Come this way."

Pirandello followed her along a narrow path he had made himself, which led to a wide, open meadow full of bristly grass. In the distance he could see small groups of passengers beginning their trek back to civilization. "I was on the train that stopped," Orlando explained, "and I've been helping some of the passengers find their belongings. The sudden stop tossed a number of items into this meadow."

"Aren't you going back with the others?" Pirandello asked.

The girl sighed. "There's nothing back there for me," she said. "I learned just yesterday that my parents had been raising me just for my long, silken hair."

"I don't mean to contradict you," Pirandello said, "but you hardly have any hair at all."

"It's being used to weave a blanket," Orlando said sadly, running her fingers through her stubble. "My parents cut it off with a long, sharp knife, which they then planned on using to cut my life short."

"That's dreadful," Pirandello said. "Dreadful and shocking."

"Dreadful and shocking and wasteful," Orlando replied. "After all, my hair will grow out again, and they could use it to make another blanket. In any case, I managed to escape them by jumping out the window. I ran right to the train station and boarded the first train that arrived. I had no idea where I was going, but now it seems I've gone here, to this forest. It's not bad here, actually. It's very peaceful."

"It *is* peaceful," Pirandello agreed, "although the food can get a little monotonous."

"Well, perhaps we're in luck," Orlando said. "At the far end of the meadow are three unclaimed objects from the train accident. I thought someone from railway safety should know about them. The first is an enormous sack of sour gummy bears."

"Egad!" Pirandello said. "I never thought such an item would end up here in the forest!"

"I know what you mean," Orlando said. "All my life I've felt like a tiny, minor character in a much larger and confusing story. I assumed that the treats in such a story would end up in the mouths of the heroes, not minor characters such as myself."

"Maybe we're not such minor characters after all," said Pirandello. "What are the two other unclaimed items?"

"See for yourself," Orlando said, for by now they were at the edge of the meadow, and Pirandello saw for himself. The first item was a large slab of wood, lying flat on the grass where it had fallen. The wood was polished to a shine that caught the morning sun and was no doubt confusing some of the cawing ravens. Toward one of its edges was a round silver knob. Pirandello had to look at the object for quite some time before he could tell what it was.

"It's a door!" he said.

"Precisely," she said. "It doesn't appear to have been part of the train, as there's no indication it was ripped off during the accident. It's just a door. Who on earth would be looking for a door?"

Pirandello did not know the answer to this question, but even if he did, he wouldn't have answered, because the third and last unclaimed item in the meadow was so strange that he simply stood and stared for quite some time, and the eerie object stared back. After all his melancholy time alone in the forest, feeling like a minor character in someone else's story, Pirandello began to feel as if he might not be alone, not with his new friend, Orlando, and that he might not be a minor character, now that this item, which surely must have been as important as it was strange, had come into his possession.

It was, of course, a head.

PROMISES, PROMISES, AND MORE PROMISES

✦ ✦ ✦ ✦ ✦

PATRICIA C. AND FREDRICK L. MCKISSACK

illustrated by CALEF BROWN

Hold on! Wait just one minute," shouted Genius Kelly, making the universal sign for *time-out*. "I am so confused right now. I don't know which way to go or how to find the head or the door!"

"I feel the same way," said Joe. "I know a lot more than I did when we started, but I don't think we're any closer to solving the problem."

"We can't give up," said Nancy. "We've gotten help from so many people along the way. We have to find Roberta's head or her systems will blow soon. And then we'll never rescue Mom and Dad." Nancy sniffed the air as if she might smell up a clue.

Nancy was the same — smart, brave, and a born leader, but everybody had noticed a difference in her. She had been acting strangely over the past few days . . . well, really since the wolf attack. First, the wound healed quickly, very quickly. Then she was stronger and could run faster than before. Her sense of smell was keener, and she had a ferocious appetite. Nancy was changing, but into what? Joe was watching his sister closely, dreading what she might be becoming.

Genius Kelly looked at his red arrow. "Look!" he exclaimed, leaping to his feet. "My arrow is spinning. It's never done that before."

"Mine is, too," said Nancy.

"And mine," Joe put in. "All our arrows are spinning counterclockwise — backward."

"The arrows are telling us that in order to go forward, we must go back to the beginning!" said Genius Kelly.

"The beginning of what? Where?" Roberta asked.

Nobody had an idea, until Angel spoke. "Ask yourselves, What was the beginning of this drama?"

"We got the birthday card from Mom and Dad on our

eleventh birthday," said Joe. "I still have it in my pocket, along with the key."

"And then what happened?" Roberta asked.

"We were escaping on a train when it blew up. We survived and ran into the woods, where the adventure began," Nancy answered. Then as if a lightbulb had gone on in her head, Nancy blurted out, "That's where we should go — back to the accident in our time and space."

Suddenly, the arrows stopped spinning.

"I think we're onto something," said Genius Kelly.

"Let's be on our way," said Hathi.

"I don't think we can or should go with them," said Sybil. "I foresee only Nancy, Joe, and Genius Kelly leaving the village on this journey."

"It makes sense," agreed Roberta. "The three of them were actually there. We weren't. So, they must go back to find the head and the door alone. We will wait for them here in the village where it is somewhat safe."

"Didn't we have this conversation before?" said Angel. "Didn't we decide that going back to stop the explosion wasn't such a good idea?"

"True," said Genius Kelly. "But we're not going to time-travel back to the past. We are returning in the here and now, looking for clues that might have been overlooked after the accident. You weren't looking for heads and doors at that time."

"Look! Our arrows are pointing north now," said Nancy.

"But the way back is south!" Joe pointed toward the woods behind the village. "On second thought," he added, "north does look like a better route."

"It might take you longer," Sybil said after peering into her ball, "but the way appears to be clear. No great obstacles."

None of the group really wanted to see Nancy and Joe go off with the pig as their only protection, but nobody challenged Genius Kelly because he had been sent by the twins' parents to protect them at all cost. And he had done his job. Besides, who had a better idea for looking for the door and the head?

After heartfelt good-byes and promises to be careful, the boy, the girl, and the big pig prepared for their trek. "We're off to the here-and-now place where the train wreck occurred," said Nancy.

"We'll wait for your return," said Sybil. Then she whispered to the three, "Please hurry. Roberta's circuits could go any minute."

"We love you," said Hathi, wiping away tears.

Angel waved, and Roberta wished them well.

Their first night out, the threesome traveled by following the North Star, steadily moving, rarely talking. At dawn, they stopped in a clearing and ate the sandwiches Angel had made from the cradle. Then they fell asleep.

Joe was awakened at nightfall by a feeling that Nancy was not there with them.

"Nancy," Joe called to the darkness. No answer.

Genius Kelly woke up. "What? What's wrong? Nancy? What?"

"She's not here," Joe whispered, fear rising in his voice.

Genius Kelly was already moving up the hill behind the clearing. Suddenly, the pig stopped in his tracks. Joe stifled a scream when he saw his sister surrounded by a pack of wolves.

Joe and Genius inched closer, crawling on their stomachs. Nancy wasn't aware of their presence. The wolves were licking her hands. Their tails were wagging like playful puppies. She looked like she was having the time of her life.

"Oh, no!" Joe shrieked. "My sister has turned into a werewolf."

"Oh, forevermore, Joe. I have not turned into a monster," Nancy said, calling over her shoulder as if she'd known they were there all the time. "Come on up here. You two need to hear this."

Genius Kelly spoke up. "It's an old urban legend, that once a person is bitten by a wolf, that person becomes a werewolf."

"Glad to hear you say that," said Nancy. The wolves began to howl and bay their agreement.

Nancy explained. "The wolves told me they are furious with the aliens for using their bodies without permission. Then the aliens did awful things, further adding to the bad reputation wolves have been trying to dispel for centuries. Granite, the alpha wolf, told me that their kind had almost been hunted to extinction because humans misunderstood them. Stories about the big, bad wolf that ate pigs, swallowed grandmothers, and turned people into werewolves didn't help either."

"How did they tell you all this?" Joe asked. He was amazed at how the wolves sat quietly while Nancy was speaking. Granite sat at her feet, looking up at her respectfully.

"Granite told me that the bite put wolf DNA in my system. It allows me to communicate with real wolves but for a limited time only. The wolves said they need a human ally to help them regain support. I told them I would speak for them if they'd help us find a head and a door."

She patted Granite on his head. The wolf raised his nose and released a sound that started deep in his belly and rose up through his throat into a perfect howl in the key of A. It was beautiful. A chorus of his pack responded with yips and growls, all communicating what was readily understood as joy.

Then Joe saw Nancy raise her own head and release her own yowl. It sounded like music. Joe was so taken with the chorus, he decided to join. So he threw back his head and let out a loud howl.

The wolves fell silent. Only the wind stirred in the trees.

"What?" said Joe, looking at Granite. Then Nancy. "What?"

"He means well," Nancy told Granite. "His insult wasn't deliberate." Then turning to Joe, she whispered, "You told the wolves that they sounded like a pack of sick geese."

Genius Kelly roared with laughter.

Joe shrugged. "Wolfese isn't my first language, you know."

Granite led his pack away, but not before he returned to nudge Nancy's hand with his nose and make a few whimpering sounds. She patted his massive back and said, "Yes. A promise is a promise. I will keep mine. Thank you."

The pack was gone and the three travelers sat on the crest of the hill sharing what they had just experienced.

"I'm a lone pig, in the woods, surrounded by wolves, and I'm still here to tell the story." Genius Kelly touched his head, his legs, and his rump to make sure all his parts were in place. He was delighted that they were.

"I can't believe my sister was conversing with wolves as if they were all best friends," Joe said, shaking his head in amazement.

"And I can't believe what Granite came back to tell me," said Nancy, laughing. "On the other side of this hill is a path. It leads to a railroad employee's tin shack about two miles away. Granite said he wasn't sure if this was useful information or not — he had no idea — but the pack saw a man and an almost-bald-headed woman take a head and a door inside the shack."

"Think of it!" shouted Joe. "We know where the head and door are!"

"Why are we sitting here talking about how amazed we are?" Genius Kelly said, hopping to his feet. "Let's get going."

So they did.

They followed Granite's directions and found the tin shack. "Check the mailbox," suggested Genius Kelly. "It can give us a lot of information about who lives here."

On the mailbox was a sign: *Pirandello's Place. 000 The Boondocks 00555.*

Nancy marched up to the front door. "Wow, does this look out of place," she whispered. "Something smells fishy here."

"Maybe we're in time for lunch," said Joe hopefully.

"No, that's not the fishy I'm talking about. This door doesn't fit this house."

She knocked on the door. It opened. "Hi! My name is Pirandello. This is my abode. You're not at all what I thought you'd be like, but you are welcome anyhow. I have fresh fish stew if you'd like to share a meal with me."

"We appreciate your hospitality," said Genius Kelly, looking equally as surprised as Nancy was by Pirandello's familiarity.

"Oh, I've been expecting you," said Pirandello. "You've come for the head or the door, or both. Right?"

Nancy gasped! "What? Who told you?" she asked.

"I'll take some of your fish stew, please," said Joe. Nancy gave him the sister look.

"When my friend Orlando and I found the head and door and the gummy bears, I knew we had something that could make me be one of the special people in the world!"

"But what made you think a head and a door had value?" Nancy asked.

Pirandello closed his eyes as if thinking how to express his thoughts. "I had a feeling. . . . I mean this head looks like it belongs to something smart — not regular smart, but super smart. Whoever has the rest of it is bound to want its head in the worst kinda way. And a door! Now doors normally lead into or out of a place. This door isn't attached to anything. But it has two sides. Whoever is on the other side of the door is gonna want to come in or get out. So I waited, figuring somebody would be coming for the head, the door, or both. I was right, and now I'm gonna cash in."

"Cash in?" said Genius Kelly.

"Well, well, well, a talking pig," said Pirandello. "Now, that's a million dollars in the bank for sure."

"Okay, guys, you heard that — a million dollars for me!" Genius Kelly made a dramatic stage bow.

Pirandello filled a bowl of stew for Joe, while Genius Kelly began to negotiate. "Are those sour gummy bears in the jar on the counter?"

Pirandello grabbed the jar as if to protect it. "Yes! I love them, so it takes a lot of discipline to eat just one a day to make them last as long as I can. So, sorry, I can't offer you one. Orlando rejected my proposal of marriage and took a train to California because I refused to share my gummy bears with her. Oh, well."

"May we see the head and the door?" asked Genius Kelly.

"Let's look at the head first." Pirandello went to a

cabinet and brought back the head as he had found it. "This will cost you five hundred thousand dollars. Cash!"

"We don't have that kind of money," argued Nancy.

"Surely, you don't expect me to give it to you. Free? Look! This is my opportunity to be famous for something. I've lived a dull, gray existence. I feel in my gut that this head is a part of something big, and I want in."

"Tell you what," said Genius Kelly, leaning back. Nancy marveled at how quickly he was able to find a point to negotiate. "You're right. You are part of an adventure. And when it is over, we are probably going to be asked by a major publishing house to write the story. If you give us the head and door, we will include an entire chapter about you in our book!"

"I'd be in a book?" said Pirandello wistfully. "I'd be famous for sure if I appear in a book . . . especially if it's a bestseller! Wow! That's worth it."

"So we can have the door and the head?" Nancy asked.

"No. Just the head . . . for your promise to put me in the book. So, promise?"

"Promise," said all three.

And that's how they got Roberta's head, rushed back to the village, and put it in place before her systems corrupted.

"Now we need to go back and negotiate for the door," said Joe. "I hope he has more stew."

"Pirandello probably has the door well hidden," said Sybil.

"Actually, Pirandello is hiding it in plain view," answered Nancy with a smile and a soft yip and yawl.

WHEN IS A DOOR
NOT A DOOR?

✦ ✦ ✦ ✦ ✦

NATALIE BABBITT

illustrated by TIMOTHY BASIL ERING

Nancy and Joe and Genius Kelly began their journey back to find a door, and as they picked their way along, Nancy told them more about her conversation with the wolves. "They're very brave, you know," she said, "and very strong and loving. Why, they claim that there've been times when wolf families have saved and raised human children from the time they were babies! They *love* families! That's the way they hunt, mostly — mother, father, and pups, all together!"

Genius snorted. "Pigs like families, too, you know," he said. "There's nothing so all-fired special about *that!*"

"You're probably right," said Joe. "But maybe the wolves know something about *our* family — our mother and father. Did you ask them, Nancy?"

"Sure," she said, "and I think they do know something. But they didn't say much. It was kind of as if they were keeping a secret. The one thing they did tell me, though, was that we had to have a door — that a door would be grand for opening the way to finding our own family. They claimed there's a new store around here in the woods somewhere with a big sign on the front that says GRAND OPENING! It sells doors mostly, but lots of other things made out of wood, and they said it's owned and operated by a dormouse."

Joe giggled. "Did they mean a door mouse, two words, or a dormouse, one word?" he asked.

"Never mind how many words," said Genius. "This mouse had better be *big*. Otherwise we'll never be able to get through the doors it uses! And anyway, I was just wondering: do they actually need doors?"

"Sometimes, I should think," said Nancy. "If they're inside and need to get out."

"Or outside and need to get in," said Joe.

And so they rattled on and on, paying no attention to the route they were taking, and didn't notice that there were more and more trees as they went along, with less and less room between for walking. The light grew dimmer, too, with so many leafy limbs above them, shutting out the afternoon sun. And then, all at once, after another hour or so — and after a noisy but unresolved argument about whether or not kangaroos in far-off Australia had to use doors that opened and closed upside down — there was a very bright patch of light up ahead. And they found as they came nearer that a large space had been cleared of trees, and a clean-looking, new-looking building was before them — a long, low building that seemed to be more of a warehouse than a store. And, yes, it had a sign, painted on a wide white strip of fabric that said in big letters: GRAND OPENING! But it had something else on it as well: a human foot painted below the lettering, with a red arrow on its little toe that pointed down toward the building's door — yes, it had a door, a door that was shut — and an invitation on a sort of poster: *This Is the Place.*

"Oh, Joe, look at that!" said Nancy in a breathless voice. "Do you think *this* place can be the real place? The place we're supposed to find the real door we're meant to bring back? There's something strange about it — but if it's right, maybe we've finally . . . well, *almost,* anyway . . . come close to finding Mom and Dad at last!"

The door to the building swung open then, with a welcoming swish, and a furry but well-combed creature in a striped apron stood there on strong hind legs. If this was a dormouse, she was more like a squirrel than a mouse — a whole lot bigger than a regular mouse and bushier in the tail — and she was munching on peanuts that she kept pulling out of her apron pocket. "How do you do, my dears!" she said. "Won't you come in, please, all of you? We're having a sale today on wooden shoes with souls."

"What sort of soul does a wooden shoe have?" asked Joe as they trooped into the building.

"Firm," she told him. "And solid. The soul of a wooden shoe will never ever bend, give in, or wear out. That's true of regular soles as well, of course, if you know what I mean. By the way, my name is Doris. I'm named for my mother *and* my grandmother! It's a good name if you're a dormouse. Everyone calls me by my name, and you may, too. What names do *you* go by?"

"I'm Joe," he told her, "and that's my twin sister, Nancy. And this pig here is our guardian, Genius Kelly."

Nancy curtsyed politely to the dormouse, and Genius tried hard to bow, but this is not easy if you've got four legs. It turned into more of a bob of the head than a bow. Still, everyone smiled, and then Nancy looked around at the store, at all the shelves holding all the items made from wood. "This is an amazing store," she said to Doris. "You have a lot of lovely things for sale. We're looking in particular for —"

But Doris interrupted her. "The store has been a great success, out here in the woods," she said proudly, gazing about. "In fact, I'm thinking of setting up a few branches. Why, Sybil Hunch, the famous misfortune-teller, comes in here all the time to buy truth-picks and close-pins. She goes through a lot of them every month and always needs more. But I keep plenty of them on hand for her, you may be sure of that. One of these days, I'll be able to talk her into buying a trunk to store them in. That way, she'll be sure not to run out. I've got some dandy trunks in the basement. How are *you* fixed for trunks, you three? Being out in the woods like this makes trunks an easy item to collect. We take the bark off ours, though, and hollow them out, and then put lids on some of them. Is that what you're after? Trunks?"

"Well, no, not exactly," said Genius, "although I'm sure they're fine for the purpose. What *we* have to have is a —"

"Birthday presents are fine here, too," said Doris, interrupting again. "I love to give my friends the dog carvings. Dogs standing up, sitting, lying down . . . you know.

Smiling, sleeping, whatever you want. They're carved from dogwood, of course — beautiful wood, dogwood — and the artist always finds a way to leave some of the bark on, somewhere, just to make a nice touch. Of course, they look a lot like wolves, some of them, but there's nothing wrong with that, you know. Here's an idea. Just leave me your names and addresses, and the dates of your birthdays, and I'll send along a card for you to order with!"

"Well," said Joe, in an effort to be polite, "since Nancy and I are twins, we have the same birthday. Write us down as Joe and Nancy Sloppy —"

But no sooner had he said these words than a sudden thundering racket burst from the back of the store — a banging and slamming, like trees falling down all around them, like a cyclone in a lumberyard, that went on and on and made them cover their ears with their hands in an effort to shut it out. Doris went running to the place from which the noise was coming, to try to make it stop, but it did no good. And soon she was back, screaming, "They've all gone crazy — all the doors! They keep slamming and bursting open, over and over — all but one! The big blue one! I just don't understand! There's a big voice like a *giant's* voice back there, yelling at that one blue door, telling it to *shut up*, but I can't see where it's *coming* from! The voice, I mean! It's just — in the *air*! I tried to block them all open, all the doors, so they'd quit slamming shut, but that one door, the blue one — there's just no way to open it! I couldn't get near enough to really see, but it looked as if someone had banged close-pins into the hinges!"

Nancy cried, "Let me take a look!" And she ran to the back of the store. Here there were doors of all kinds and colors leaning in their frames against the wall, and all were bursting open and banging shut — all except a big blue one. Its hinges and knocker and knob were shiny brass, and above the mail slot were the initials *A. S.* "Alistair Sloppy!" she cried. "Joe! Come look! It's father's door! Help me get it open!"

But the giant voice protested, drowning her own words out: "It stands for *Always Shut! A* FOR *Always, S* FOR *Shut!*" And as her hand reached out, it warned her in its booming voice, "IF YOU TOUCH THAT DOORKNOB, IT WILL BE THE END FOR YOU!" And the big blue door itself, as if it were straining against the close-pins, made a yearning, groaning noise. And then all fell silent. The other doors stopped opening and closing; the giant voice was stilled. And Nancy stood there helpless, trying her very best to keep from weeping.

"Que Será, Será"

♦ ♦ ♦ ♦ ♦

JACK GANTOS

illustrated by CHRIS VAN DUSEN

The moment everything went silent, Doris the dormouse became very nervous. Silence was a kind of void in which her thoughts became lost like wooden needles in a wooden haystack. It was only through hearing herself speak that she knew what she was thinking, and because she was so squirrely, even for a dormouse, she nervously began to sing in a voice that was not unlike the sharp siren of a forest-fire alarm.

"*Que será, será!*" she wailed with her little arms reaching toward the ever-expanding universe, "Whatever will be, will be. The future's not ours to see. *Que será, será.*"

Genius Kelly finished off the final line of the verse, "What will be, will be."

Joe and Nancy felt left out. "What are you singing about?" they asked in unison.

Genius Kelly looked at them as if their IQs had suddenly dropped a hundred points and failed to bounce. "We are singing about *fate*," he said condescendingly. "About not knowing what the future will be yet having to accept without disappointment what the future will offer each one of us."

"But what if the future is not made of wood?" Doris asked in a voice near to tears.

Everyone ignored her.

"Are you saying this bulging blue door is part of our fate?" Nancy asked Genius.

"Could I spell this out any more clearly?" he replied, exasperated with Nancy and Joe because his thinking was so much more advanced.

"Then why can't we just open the door," Joe suggested with great earnestness, "and embrace our fate with open arms?" He reached forward and grabbed the doorknob.

"Because," Genius said in a tone of voice that was electric with concern, "fate is not always your friend." He deftly speared Joe's hand with his pig's foot and jerked it away.

"But our parents might be right behind the door," cried Nancy. "And they might be thinking it is their fate that we open the door so they can embrace us. I would even go back and live in the circus again with that evil clown if we were all together as a family. I'd even live in one of those greasy little circus wagons, which I've always thought are creepy and airless and overcrowded with pieces of broken furniture and dusty-looking fake plants and a relative who is always lingering in the corner as he sharpens a long, sharp knife."

"I feel the same way," agreed Joe. "Plus, I'd even polish all those gigantic red clown shoes again and rake up elephant dung with a smile on my face if Mom and Dad would return."

"I may not be the sharpest knife in the drawer," Doris interjected. "I mean, I can whittle a wooden chain out of a two-by-four, and a nuclear submarine out of a massive redwood, but I know that your lives are forever changed. There is no going back to the past. My last store was all items made of aluminum cans. It was a gleaming palace of pop-top-shelf merchandise until the recycling craze put me out of business. And before that failure, I had a doomed plant store where I sold canisters of greenhouse gasses. So I know that change is a one-way street. There is no going back."

"I agree," Joe said with authority, and once more he reached for the doorknob. "So let's go forward!"

And once more Genius Kelly stabbed his hand away.

"Just why don't you want us to open the door?" asked Joe, rubbing the pain from his knuckles.

"Yes," added Nancy. "I thought you were on our side. But now I smell a rat." She gave the pig a suspicious look. "Perhaps you've never wanted us to find our parents."

"I assure you," Genius Kelly replied with great calmness, "that you do not smell a rat. I am fully on your side. My duty is to protect you and to see to it that you find your parents and to not suffer a tragic death along the way."

"Death?" jabbered Doris as she nervously picked splinters from her chin. "Who said anything about death?"

Everyone ignored her.

"I have no intention of dying," stated Nancy.

"But if you do," interjected Doris, "I have a lovely hand-carved mahogany coffin that comes in your size, with a variety of colorful bark liners."

"Please," Genius Kelly begged, "let us stay on task. Now,

follow my thinking here. Look at the door. Do you see the mail slot?"

"Yes," they said in robotic unison.

"Now look closely at what is oozing out of it," said Genius.

They all dropped to their knees and reached for the whitish, yellowish goop that was slowly seeping from the mail slot.

"Don't touch it!" Genius instructed. "These drips are the advance scouts of an Eggy-Thing invasion force."

"And, Mr. Genius," Doris said, "how could you possibly know that?"

"Put two and two together," Genius replied. "Bacon and eggs! Every pig has been taught from birth to know that the smell of an egg means doom for our porcine breed."

This stunningly sad piece of information seemed so true that all four of our characters shared one collective thought. How is it, they pondered in silent unison, that children learn their morals, ethics, and values from early children's books populated with clever and cute animals, which they, the readers, later learn to eat? They were galvanized with this revelation but not frozen by it because the clattering mail slot snapped them to attention, and right away they saw that through the slot the Eggy-Thing ooze began to spit out toward them with phlegmy tendrils that seemed to reach for their legs.

"It is happening," Genius said gravely. "The very worst thing you might imagine is about to take place if that door is not completely sealed."

"But if we seal it, we will never get to our parents!" shouted Nancy in despair.

"And if you don't seal it, your fate will be sealed for good," replied Genius. "And if your parents are alive, then they will have no chance of rescuing you. What would be worse? They find you dead, or you find them dead?"

It was a terrible question.

"I'd rather they find me dead," Joe said heavily, then dropped his chin onto his chest and stared at the exotic heartwood floorboards.

"Pull out of it," Nancy said to Joe as she gave Genius a harsh look. "We aren't living in an either-or world at the moment. The world we are living in has multiple —"

But Doris, who needed to speak again in order to know she was still alive, said, "Then help me with these coffins!" Quickly she bounded across the store and grabbed the end

of one with her super dormouse strength. Joe followed, and soon they had picked it up and set it in front of the door and blocked the mail slot, which pinched down on some of the Eggy-Thing goop. A faint cry could be heard from behind the door, but Doris, Genius, Nancy, and Joe were in no mood to empathize with the enemy. Quickly they stacked another coffin on top of the first, and another until you couldn't see the blue door at all.

"Get the wood glue and fasten the coffins to the door," Doris instructed Genius. "We'll seal them up in a crypt."

But Genius was nowhere to be seen.

"Genius Kelly!" shouted Joe.

"Where are you?" hollered Nancy.

"Does anyone smell bacon?" asked Doris.

They ignored her.

The twins ran toward the front door of the shop of wood, and they could just make out the pink curly tail of Genius as he slipped between two distant trees.

"He's onto something," Nancy said. "Hurry up."

"There is a law of physics that Sir Isaac Newton discovered," Joe said, suddenly remembering. He had a talent for uniting random facts. "For every action, there is a reaction — and for every front door there is a back door."

"Pirandello's door!" exclaimed Nancy. "That must be where he is heading."

You would think pigs would be slow, but Genius was not all lard. He was made of sausage and chops and other muscular cuts. He dashed through the undergrowth of the forest as if he were sniffing out truffles. The twins followed as best they could, but before long they lost him and managed to get themselves lost in the process. There they stood, in the middle of a forest, with not a path in sight and no possible way to contact the outside world.

Nancy hung her head. "All fate is loneliness," she said, quoting her favorite nursery rhyme.

"We live as we dream — alone," moaned Joe, quoting someone famous who went up a river in the Congo and got stupidly lost. "We are all alone and doomed," he said, and felt faint.

"No, we are not," Nancy shouted. "Look!" She pointed at the floor of the forest. There in the dirt was drawn the outline of a toe with an arrow on it.

"I guess that's why they call him a genius," said Joe.

"Follow that toe," cried Nancy with her hopes fully restored. "We must get to that back door."

"Is it a full moon tonight?" Joe asked as he ran.

Nancy looked up into the still-blue sky. "Can't tell yet," she said. "Why?"

"I fear a high tide," Joe replied. "An Eggy-Thing high tide that might surge from door to door."

And off they ran. "Genius!" they kept crying out. "Wait for us!"

THE FINAL SCRAMBLE

✦ ✦ ✦ ✦ ✦

M. T. ANDERSON
illustrated by JAMES RANSOME

It was a terrible and frantic night in those woods. The wind blew through the trees. It smelled of sulfur . . . or eggs. The trees tossed back and forth, as if whisking an omelet in the thick, yolk-scented air.

On one side of the woods, the twins scampered through pines toward Pirandello's shack. They were searching for their interstellar pig protector. And on the other side of the wood, a motley band wandered through poplar trees: a witchy gypsy, a pirate named Angel, and a bobble-headed robot riding on a circus elephant. They, too, were searching for their friends — for the twins, the pig, the whole lot.

And in the middle of the woods, in the Grand Opening's storeroom, tides of spattery, splattery, batter-y creatures thrashed against the door to their world. The creatures had hoped that Nancy and Joe could be tricked into opening the door. Now, as a result of the timely intervention of that clever porker Genius Kelly, the gloppy invaders had to beat the door down. They frothed and splashed in waves against the barrier of epoxied coffins.

And in another part of the wood, all the Eggy-Things in their costumes — gorillas, irritable elephants, suited wolves, and one angry clown — were beginning to come to themselves after having been dismissed by Angel's power. They were growling on walkie-talkies to their friends on the other side of the door. They were marching there to let their goopy friends into this world. For years they had prepared to invade through the holes that Alistair Sloppy had opened up. And now this very night was the moment for the grand attack.

The Eggy-Things told each other dorky, dumb jokes about how the humans were soon going to submit to their rule — "Soon, the *yolk* will be on them!" they said, and, "I know! It really *cracks me up!*" And this was the most terrible thing of all: even old, lame puns like these made them quiver and tremble with hideous, slurpy laughter, boiling with insane, hysterical giggles.

The future eggy rulers of the earth had an awful sense of humor. The trees rocked back and forth above them while they howled with laughter and with their own sense of future victory.

Meanwhile, Joe and Nancy hopped along paths, guided by marks Genius Kelly had left on the ground.

"You think . . ." huffed Joe, "that Genius Kelly has gone back to Pirandello's shack?"

"Yes!" said Nancy. "I think the door on Pirandello's shack — that's the door our parents are behind! That's where they are!"

"I hope you're right," said Joe. "They owe me ten years of back allowance."

They came over a rise and saw the shack in front of them. In the distance, the train tracks on tall trestles were outlined against the evening sky. One had been shattered by the explosion of a bomb.

Genius Kelly was arguing with Pirandello.

"I am not paying you ten thousand dollars for your door."

Pirandello swung the door open and closed. It shut with a satisfying click. "Mmm," said Pirandello. "That is one great door. Let me just hear that click again." He was about to open it again, infuriatingly, when he stopped himself. "Oh, never mind. I can do it later, once you've left. Because it's my door. Mine. And you can't use it unless you buy it for fifteen thousand dollars."

"Fifteen!" cried Genius Kelly.

"You don't appreciate what an incredible door this is," said Pirandello. "But I'm not going to sit here bickering with you, throwing pearls before swine. . . . Oh, sorry. Present company excepted."

Genius Kelly was exasperated. "We need that door! There's no time to lose!"

"You're telling me," said Pirandello, looking at his pocket watch. "There's a train scheduled to come through in ten minutes, and it's going to fly off that broken, bombed-out bridge you see up there if I don't signal the conductor to stop in time. So this is no time to haggle about money." He held out his hand. "Ten thousand dollars and we'll call it a deal."

"Please," said Nancy, "please, Pirandello! We just want to *use* the door! We don't even need to keep it once we've used it!"

"See? That's what that Orlando girl said about my gummy bears. Just going to use them, then she'd give them back when she was done with them." He shook his head. "I know, right?" He frowned. "I still miss her. But . . . but — as they say, where one door closes, another one opens. And in this case, the door that opens is mine, mine, mine."

Genius Kelly said, "This is ridiculous. You just found this door!"

"Finders, keepers."

Nancy pleaded, "Let us use it for ten minutes."

"Losers, weepers."

Genius Kelly said, "It's to save their parents!"

"You know my price."

"Too bad," said Joe. "Too bad — that it's not your door at all. And I can prove it."

The others stared at him. He smiled slyly and reached into his pocket. He pulled out the key that they'd found earlier — the key they were given by Angel, the magical pirate — the key Joe had fought a squid for on the sea floor. Joe said to Pirandello, "If it's your door, why is it that you can't lock it or unlock it? Why is it that I can, I bet? With this key?"

Pirandello sucked his teeth. "That key?" He realized he was beaten.

"This key."

Pirandello looked at the key. He looked at the door. He said, "Okay. Fifteen dollars. Yours for fifteen dollars."

"It's our door," Joe said.

Pirandello said, "Ten dollars. I want to buy a train ticket. I want to go find Orlando and offer her half the bag of gummy bears. To eat and then keep."

At this, Nancy's heart melted. "Oh, let's give him the ten dollars!"

"Orlando and I could be very happy in this shack," said Pirandello miserably. "Although it will be cold without a door."

"We'll leave the door when we're done with it," Joe promised. He walked to the door and inserted the key. It fit perfectly, of course. Joe stared at the silver knob. He looked at his sister, his eyes round with awe.

"When you turn that key," said Nancy, "it will free our parents! I just know it!"

"This is very exciting," said Genius Kelly. "I'm tired of babysitting. I deserve some slops on the other side of the space-time continuum."

Joe started to unlock the door. Then he stopped. He held out his hand to Nancy. Nancy took it.

Together, brother and sister Sloppy turned the key in the lock of the door. They heard the tumblers tumble. They heard the sneck unsnick.

And nothing happened. The door just unlocked.

They opened it. They saw Pirandello's cot. Everyone stared in dismay at the inside of the hut. The kids were dismayed because their parents weren't there on the other side. Pirandello was dismayed because he wished he'd cleaned up his socks before he had guests.

Nancy slumped. "Oh, no," she said. "It didn't do a thing! It's not a special interdimensional door at all!"

"But the key fit!" Genius Kelly protested. "Your parents should be here, dragging you away from porcine day care and off into the sunset — which is happening very picturesquely behind that ruined railroad trestle!"

"Yes," said Pirandello. "That railroad trestle. I do have to pop along and make sure that the train that's coming in a few minutes doesn't —"

"This is terrible!" said Nancy. "What do we do?"

Joe stewed. "Wait," he said. "Remember that vision that Sybil Hunch had in her crystal ball? She saw the key being turned in the door — by —"

"Yes!" said Nancy. "By — by —"

"Roberta the robot," said Roberta the robot, riding into the clearing on Hathi. She rattled atop the elephant. Angel and Sybil Hunch ran alongside. Sybil cackled with delight to see the children again. Hathi trumpeted. And Roberta said, "Pip, pip. I believe you're looking for me?"

"Roberta!" Nancy exclaimed. "You're just in time!"

The robot slithered down the trunk of the friendly elephant. She clanked over to the door.

"Here you go, miss," said Joe, handing her the key. Sometimes — when it mattered — Joe was very polite.

"And so, ten years later, I fulfill my purpose," said Roberta.

She shut the door. She stuck the key in the lock. She turned the key. She tugged at the knob.

And the door opened while staying closed. That's how it looked — the door doubling somehow, like two doors, in two worlds. One was solid, and one was transparent. One was opened, and the other was closed.

And standing there, in the doorway, with their ears pressed to the spot where the door had been, were Alistair and Libby Sloppy. They were older now than they had been. Their hair was a little gray, and their faces were a little lined. Behind them was a world of swirling colors.

"Children!" they gasped. "Joe! Nancy!" They rushed out, with open arms. "You know who we are, right?"

It had been ten years, but now the long separation was over. There were embraces all around. Daddy Sloppy hugged his daughter, and Libby Sloppy hugged her son. Then they switched, and Joe Sloppy hugged his father, while Nancy Sloppy slung her arms around her mom. They hardly knew one another — and yet, here they were, a family, together once more.

This would be a highly touching scene — and you would hear lots about how they all told each other stories of life in the circus caravan, recounting tales about the days spent learning the tightrope walk and the nights spent jumping from striped poles, or, for the Sloppy parents, the endless days trapped outside of time and space, listening to the sloshing of Eggy-Things trying to squidge their way into our world — but a shadow fell across this first embrace.

It was the shadow of wolves.

They arose around the little group.

"The wolves!" said Nancy. "Oh, Mom, Dad, by the way, I'm becoming part wolf, incidentally."

Her father muttered, "Next time we leave, we have got to find a better day-care situation."

Nancy said, "Don't worry. I think being part wolf will make me a better circus act."

Libby Sloppy put her hand on her forehead. "You say you don't mind becoming a werewolf because you'll do better in the circus." She sighed. "We have not been very good parents. We have a lot of making up to do . . . and a lot of catching up to do."

The wolves growled to Nancy.

Nancy listened. "They say . . . they say that the Eggy-Things in costumes have gone and unlocked the door in the Grand Opening. The others who were waiting are pouring through. They'll be here any minute!"

Another wolf growled some more.

"Oh," said Nancy to Pirandello. "And there's some other news. This wolf, Virginia, says she saw your friend Orlando. Orlando's still in the woods."

"So it's not all bad news!" said Pirandello, delighted. He threw his arms around Virginia Wolf. "If life gives you lemons, make lemonade!"

"Or," said Alistair Sloppy sharply, "if life gives you eggs, make an omelet. They'll be here any second. Eggy-Things. Thousands of them."

"Oh, yeah," said Pirandello. He looked at his watch.

"And there's a circus train due to come through anytime . . . and it's going to fall off the ruined track if I don't stop it." He looked worried.

"A circus train?" said Joe. "What do you mean?"

"The Sick and Tired Circus is going to be crossing that broken bridge in minutes."

"The Sick and Tired Circus!" said Nancy. "That's our circus!"

"The train's in danger! The Eggy-Things are coming!" said Libby Sloppy. "What will we possibly do?"

It was a bad night to reenter the world after ten years of floating outside of time and space.

And so night fell.

On one side of the forest, a train rushed through the night. A train filled with lions and elephants and clowns. And on the other side of the forest, leaping and frothing, yellow and sticky, hurling their unfried and unfriendly splattering selves through the underbrush, a tide of mucusy monsters stormed into the world.

And, gathered around a hut, near a broken train trestle, a few friends stood between an invasion of eggs and the fate of the world.

In a case like this, there was no sunny-side up.

OVER EASY

◆ ◆ ◆ ◆ ◆

KATHERINE PATERSON

illustrated by CALEF BROWN

If you have been following this adventure as closely as the authors have hoped, you will not be surprised to know that at this moment of supreme crisis, Nancy — the brave, the intelligent, the moral Nancy — took charge of the situation.

"First of all," she said, "Pirandello must stop the train." As Pirandello rushed to obey, she shouted after him, "And tell the ringmaster to set up the tent as quickly as possible with the large opening facing the woods! It's so," she explained to the others, "the aliens will come rushing in after us."

"We're going to be standing in there *waiting* for them?" Joe had always respected his sister's acumen, but somehow, running seemed a better option at the moment.

"Good thinking, Nancy," Angel said. "And we should all go now and help them set up the tent. We can do it in that grassy spot right beside the tracks. There's no time to lose."

Everyone except Genius Kelly, who was very speedy when he chose, swung up on Hathi's back, and the great beast raced toward the spot.

The train had barely shuddered to a stop when all the members of the circus had been hustled off and, led by the shouts of the ringmaster, went to work. As you can imagine, people who belong to a circus are well practiced in setting up a tent in an expeditious manner. In less time than it would take you to sing "Ninety-nine Bottles of Beer on the Wall" followed by all four verses of "The Star-Spangled Banner" (provided you know all four verses) the big top was erected.

With no time to spare, however. Indeed, Hathi and the other friendly pachyderms had barely hammered down the last tent pole when the Eggy-Things, having cast off all their disguises, came streaming through the woods and slurped into the tent at such a speed that our friends winced at the *schlap* against the canvas on the opposite side.

The ringmaster was already on the job. "Ladies, gentlemen, gentle beasts, and uh — super-ova," he cried in his best ringmaster voice. "We have, if a bit hastily, assembled for you the greatest little show on earth."

"Forget the show on earth!" one of the Eggy-Things yelled. "We want extraterrestrial jokes!"

"Ah, of course," said Angel, stepping into the ring, "but ours are old and tired and very earthy, and we need your help."

"Yes," cried Sybil Hunch. "Give us your yolks!"

"Then (yuk, yuk) the yolk will be on you, old voman! After the yolks, we'll give you our very specially imported brand of salmonella. You will die slowly and painfully, which will be fun to see, but we won't be able to linger too long. We have to spread our contagion throughout the planet." With these words of mucusy menace, the Eggy-Things started across the width of the tent toward our heroes.

"No, no!" said Joe. "Ve only vant da yolks!"

The silly ova began laughing and separating themselves, the yellows from the whites. "Toodle-oo," cried the yolks to their albuminoidal halves. "Be ready. As soon as we stop yolking around, slither hither. We gotta yob to do. Yuk, yuk." It was impossible to tell if there was one voice speaking or a multitude of voices.

"Don't worry," came the reply. "We're white behind you!"

"Not bad for ones so colorless!" said Genius Kelly in his most superior tone of voice. "But, somehow, we expect better from you yellows. If the condemned prisoner can request one last good smoke, we'd like to go out with one last good joke."

The eggy yolks couldn't bear to be sneered at by a pig and began to scramble for the honor of delivering the last good joke.

"Knock, knock!"

"Who's there?"

"Oregon."

"Oregon who?"

"Oregonna take over the world?"

"You betcha!" chorused both halves, and the yuks that followed this bad joke were so loud they shook the tent. But, to the invaders' distress, not a one of our heroes even cracked a smile. They tried again.

"Knock, knock!"

"Who's there?"

"Scieszka."

"Gesundheit!" yelled Joe, ruining the joke and annoying their enemies no end.

"No more shouting out answers!"

"I'm sorry," said Joe, "but I do want to have one last laugh before it's all over, and I'd already heard that joke."

The yolks went into a huddle. Or, for those readers familiar with the game, into a sort of rugby scrum. At last one yolk seemed to separate from the mass. There was the sound of a throat clearing. "We are going to have a joke, or, if you prefer, a yolk-off. The winner will have the honor of making the final joke."

Genius Kelly sighed loudly and pretended to examine his hoof. The elephants sighed even more loudly and lay down on the ground and pretended to snore.

"If you noodle noggins have any desire to live long enough for a last laugh, this will be your *last* chance." With that, he, she, or it ducked back into the scrum and soon there arose from that side of the tent such a cacophony of screeches and yuks that our heroes put their hands, hooves, paws, feet, or trunks over their ears in defense.

"Look!" Nancy had to yell in Joe's ear to be heard at all.

Joe looked and what he saw astounded him. The mass of yellows was going around faster and faster. The more the yolks yelled, the faster around they went. The scrum was being scrambled. "Those stupid yolks are beating themselves up!" he said.

Nancy glanced over at the waiting whites. If they had had eyes, their eyes would have been popping out. "Quick!" she cried. "Everyone go into your act. As fast as you can!"

Suddenly the Sick and Tired Circus was sick and tired no more. Genius Kelly danced and whirled into his magical judo act. The twins did loopedy loops on the high wires; the elephants swung their trunks about and then their huge rear ends with their tails a-twirling. The ringmaster spun around with his whip going at least ninety miles per hour. Roberta grabbed the hand of the headless woman, who in turn grabbed a monkey's paw, which grabbed the hand of the bearded lady, who grabbed a string of chimps, who grabbed a seal's flipper, who flapped Roberta's other hand, and they raced ring around a rosie about the startled whites, who grew paler and fuller of air by the moment. Every now and then a piteous wail arose over the racket of frenzied circus acts: "Help!" and "Stop! I'm airsick!" and even: "We'll mend our wicked ways if you'll stop whipping us!"

But no one even paused to listen. Our heroes knew better than to trust even the pallid portion of the villainous invaders. And before long all the whites had been whipped into a giant meringue, making the lions roar with delight.

"Fire-juggling act!" yelled Joe. And the clowns grabbed

the torches and juggled and breathed fire onto the newly whipped meringue until it stood up in beautiful ecru peaks.

"Scrambled eggs for a main course and a lovely meringue for dessert," said Sybil. "It looks almost good enough to eat."

"Almost," said Genius Kelly wryly.

Meanwhile Angel had been busy summoning the Cradle of Time. With the elephants' help, all the scrambled yolks were piled into the cradle and topped off by the giant meringue. For a few moments our exhausted friends watched and listened, the beasts panting, the people perspiring, but they needn't have worried. There wasn't even a whimper from the cradle. Neither the scrambled yolks nor the whipped whites showed any sign of reconstituting. The Eggy-Things that had threatened them for so long had been done in by their own rotten humor and the cleverness of our little band of heroes.

"Now, off you go," Angel said. "Back to the big bang!"

"Not so fast!" said an ominous but familiar voice. It was, of course, Boppo. He had one giant clown foot atop Libby Verrie-Sloppy and another holding Professor Alistair Sloppy on the ground. Both the twins' parents appeared to be asleep.

"They are under my power," said the evil clown. "While

the rest of you were busy whipping up trouble, I managed to hypnotize this pair with my best juggling act. It was all done with mirrors — very skillfully, if I do say so myself. Now I will rescue my comrades and throw these two into the cradle of their own making. Then I will extract from my pocket one final bomb, which will, for sentimental reasons, go off in exactly forty-seven ticks of the clock."

"Oh, no," said Joe. "Not that stupid juggling act again."

"I never trusted that red-nosed ruffian," said Hathi.

"Just when I thought misfortune had landed on its head," Sybil said sadly.

Genius Kelly gave a deeply dejected "oink."

Nancy jabbed Joe in the ribs. "Sing," she muttered.

"Huh?"

"Lullaby and good night," Nancy began softly, and then Joe and all their friends from the Sick and Tired Circus were singing along: "With roses bedight." Before they got to the third line about the lilies, Boppo had sunk to the earth with a snore.

With catlike quickness, Angel threw the evil clown and his ticking bomb into the cradle and sent him and the whole alien brunch racing toward the creation of the universe.

It all happened so fast that they simply stared at the

empty space in the sky that the cradle had flown through.

"Hurray," said a tiny voice. Everyone turned in amazement. It had come from the throat of the headless woman — her first spoken word.

A baby monkey began to clap his tiny hands, and soon they were all cheering and dancing and shouting and hugging one another in relief that the danger had passed and in joy at what they had accomplished.

And now we come to the part of the story no one likes much: the farewells between friends who have suffered and struggled and, yes, even laughed together.

Pirandello headed off to the forest, where he found Orlando munching on gummy bears and took her home. Angel and Sybil said good-bye and started off together, as Angel had become quite fond of the misfortune-teller and determined to protect her from any misfortunes that still lurked in her neighborhood.

The last departing pair was Roberta and Genius Kelly. Roberta had cleverly undone Boppo's hypnotic spell over the senior Sloppys. When their friends and ours had escorted them to the door before Pirandello's shack, the professor gave a lovely little speech, thanking the robot handsomely for all she had done, and then added, a bit sadly, "My dear, you are no longer a corpse, as exquisite as you were and are. You are free to go back to that other dimension, where you will find others of your rare kind that I constructed in my years behind the door. They will welcome you as the hero you have become. Take this wonderful pig back with you, as he and you belong in that other dimension. He will serve as a companion and reminder of all you have both done to save not only the Sloppy family, but all human and animal kind. The key that you have will take you back through the door. Please lock it behind you and throw it away, for, though the Eggy-Things no longer exist in that dimension or this one, I am convinced that there should be no more trafficking between our two worlds."

Genius Kelly raised his snout preparing, it would appear, to make a long speech, but Roberta punched him in the short ribs and smilingly urged him toward the door, though she paused on the threshold to hug the twins and say, "Now I know I have a heart, because it is breaking."

It was all Nancy could do to keep from weeping. Even brave Joe was seen to wipe away a tear.

"Wait!" said the pig. "I have to tell the twins their true names."

"Nancy and Joe are not our real names?" asked Nancy.

"No," said Genius Kelly. "Your true names"— and here he cleared his throat ceremoniously —"are Josephus and Natochka."

"What?" cried the twins in unison.

"I'm sorry, children. We repented as soon as we filed the birth certificates," said their father.

"That's why we've always called you Joe and Nancy," said their mother.

"Then is it okay if we just stay Joe and Nancy?" asked Joe.

"Perfectly okay," said their father. "Thank you, G. K., for all you have done for our children."

"May I beg a small favor?" said the pig.

"Certainly," said the Professor.

"I know it sounds preposterous, but could I have one last joke to send me on my way?"

"Knock, knock," said Joe.

"Who may I ask is calling?" replied the pig.

"G. K." said Joe.

"G. K. who?"

"Gee, Kan't you stay with us a little longer?"

A fat tear rolled down the porker's black snout. "Very good," he said, waving a hoof. "I almost wish I could, but as you know, I must return." And with that, he followed Roberta through the door, which closed soundly behind them.

Suddenly Joe, who could never remain gloomy for very long, whipped something out of his pocket. It was the birthday card that had started all their adventures. "Mom and Dad," he said, "when we got your card, we were in the middle of a very special birthday party."

"The Elephant Clown Party!" cried Nancy. "In all the excitement, I forgot about it."

"We didn't forget," said Hathi. "Come back to the tent. Everything is ready. We will give you the party of your lives."

I don't have time to tell you about the wonderful party. You'll have to use your imagination to picture clowns and elephants and seals and lions and a bearded woman and headless woman and monkeys and chimps and every person and creature determined to give the beloved twins the greatest time of their eleven years, even if in their hearts they knew it was not only a birthday bash but a farewell party.

When it was over, and Nancy and Joe turned for the last, worst good-bye, to Hathi and all their friends of the circus, the loving pachyderm said to the Sloppy parents, "There is no need for you to go. Please make your home with us. Joe and Nancy are already family."

The senior Sloppys looked at the twins and then into the pleading eyes of every person and beast assembled. "Why not?" said Professor Sloppy. "I could put my inventive mind to work among you all."

"Why not?" said Libby Verrie-Sloppy. "I've always longed to ride bareback on elephants. And I'm a terrible cook."

"Why not?" said Joe. "The villains are gone and our parents are here. That was all that was wrong with the Sick and Tired Circus — villains here and parents missing."

Nancy stroked the place on her arm where the wolf had scratched her. The house with a picket fence and two parents with their twins no longer seemed so desirable. Wasn't a circus the perfect home for a girl who was, at least for the present, part wolf? And besides, she had promised the wolves to speak out for them. "Why not?" she said.

Hathi encircled the four Sloppys with her warm trunk. "Then it's settled," she said.

I won't say it was the end of all their adventures, for Nancy and Joe were an adventurous pair, but it brings to a close the Exquisite Corpse Adventure — evil conquered, family united, and friends who lived, I'm quite sure, happily ever after.

NOTES ON CONTRIBUTORS

M. T. ANDERSON is the author of *Feed*, a National Book Award Finalist and a *Los Angeles Times* Book Prize Finalist, as well as *The Suburb Beyond the Stars*. His two volumes of *The Astonishing Life of Octavian Nothing* were both Michael L. Printz Honor Books, and *Volume I: The Pox Party* was a National Book Award winner. He is a member of the board of directors of the NCBLA.

NATALIE BABBITT is the author of *Tuck Everlasting*, an American Library Association Notable Children's Book; the Newbery Honor Book *Knee-Knock Rise*; and *Jack Plank Tells Tales*. She is a member of the board of directors of the NCBLA.

CALEF BROWN is the author-illustrator of *Dutch Sneakers and Flea Keepers*, and of *Tippintown: A Guided Tour* and *Flamingos on the Roof: Poems and Paintings*, a *New York Times* bestseller and winner of a Myra Cohn Livingston Award for Poetry.

SUSAN COOPER is the author of *Victory* and the award-winning Dark Is Rising series, including *The Dark Is Rising*, a Newbery Honor Book, and *The Grey King*, a Newbery Medal winner. She is a member of the board of directors of the NCBLA.

KATE DICAMILLO is the author of the Newbery Honor Book *Because of Winn-Dixie*; *The Tale of Despereaux*, which won the Newbery Medal; *The Magician's Elephant*; and *Bink and Gollie*.

TIMOTHY BASIL ERING is the illustrator of *The Tale of Despereaux*, winner of the Newbery Medal, as well as *Snook Alone*, and is the author-illustrator of *The Story of Frog Belly Rat Bone*.

JACK GANTOS is the author of the Rotten Ralph series and the Joey Pigza series, which includes the Newbery Honor Book *Joey Pigza Loses Control*. He is the 2010 winner of the ALAN Award for Outstanding Achievement in the Field of Adolescent Literature.

NIKKI GRIMES is the author of *Barack Obama: Son of Promise, Child of Hope; Bronx Masquerade*, winner of a Coretta Scott King Author Award; and *A Girl Named Mister*. She is a member of the board of directors of the NCBLA.

SHANNON HALE is the author of *Princess Academy*, a Newbery Honor Book and *New York Times* bestseller; *The Goose Girl*, the first in the Bayern series; and a graphic novel for young readers, *Calamity Jack*.

STEVEN KELLOGG is the illustrator of more than one hundred children's books, including *Is Your Mama a Llama?*, the Pinkerton series, and *The Pied Piper's Magic*. He is a recipient of the Regina Medal and is a vice president of the board of directors of the NCBLA.

GREGORY MAGUIRE is the author of novels for both adults and children, including *Wicked: The Life and Times of the Wicked*

Witch of the West, which was made into a hit Broadway musical; *What-the-Dickens: The Story of a Rogue Tooth Fairy*, a *New York Times* bestseller; and *Matchless: A Christmas Story*. He is an honorary board member of the NCBLA.

MEGAN McDONALD is the author of the *New York Times* best-selling Judy Moody series, as well as a book series about Judy Moody's little brother, Stink, and *The Sisters Club* series.

PATRICIA C. AND FREDRICK L. McKISSACK have cowritten more than one hundred books together, including two Coretta Scott King Author Award winners. Their titles include *A Long Hard Journey: The Story of the Pullman Porter* and *Days of Jubilee: The End of Slavery in the United States*. Patricia is also the author of *The Dark-Thirty: Southern Tales of the Supernatural*, a Newbery Honor Book. The McKissacks also collaborated with their son John McKissack to write *The Clone Codes*. They both serve on the board of directors of the NCBLA.

LINDA SUE PARK is the author of *A Single Shard*, a Newbery Medal winner; *When My Name Was Keoko*; and *Storm Warning*, Book 9 of the 39 Clues series. She is a member of the board of directors of the NCBLA.

KATHERINE PATERSON is the author of *Bridge to Terabithia* and *Jacob Have I Loved*, both winners of the Newbery Medal, as well as

The Day of the Pelican. A two-time National Book Award winner, she is the current National Ambassador for Young People's Literature and serves as a vice president of the board of directors of the NCBLA.

JAMES RANSOME is the illustrator of *The Creation,* winner of a Coretta Scott King Illustrator Award and an International Board on Books for Young People Honor Selection, and of *Uncle Jed's Barbershop,* a Coretta Scott King Illustrator Award Honor Book. He is also the author-illustrator of *Gunner, Football Hero.*

JON SCIESZKA is the author of the Time Warp Trio series, *Spaceheadz,* and *The Stinky Cheese Man and Other Fairly Stupid Tales,* a Caldecott Honor Book. He served as the first National Ambassador for Young People's Literature.

LEMONY SNICKET is the elusive author of the *New York Times* best-selling Series of Unfortunate Events books, the first three of which have been adapted into a movie. He is also the author of *The Composer Is Dead.*

CHRIS VAN DUSEN is the author-illustrator of the Mr. Magee series and *The Circus Ship,* and the illustrator of the *New York Times* best-selling Mercy Watson series, which includes *Mercy Watson Goes for a Ride,* a Theodor Seuss Geisel Honor Book.

COPYRIGHT ACKNOWLEDGMENTS

ACKNOWLEDGMENTS

The National Children's Book and Literacy Alliance (NCBLA) and the Center for the Book in the Library of Congress would like to express our deep gratitude to the many talented individuals who made *The Exquisite Corpse Adventure* an online reality leading to the development of this book. Gifted authors and illustrators M. T. Anderson, Natalie Babbitt, Calef Brown, Susan Cooper, Kate DiCamillo, Timothy Basil Ering, Jack Gantos, Nikki Grimes, Shannon Hale, Steven Kellogg, Gregory Maguire, Megan McDonald, Patricia and Fredrick McKissack, Linda Sue Park, Katherine Paterson, James Ransome, Jon Scieszka, Lemony Snicket, and Chris Van Dusen gave generously of their time and talent creating the hilarious episodes and art. Geri Zabela Eddins, Elizabeth Rock, and Eden Edwards from the NCBLA and Guy Lamolinara, John Sayers, Erin Allen, Staceya Sistare, Jane Gilchrist, and the web services team from the Library of Congress comprised our talented production team; they worked tirelessly behind the scenes to organize, design, write, edit, and promote *The Exquisite Corpse Adventure* and its websites at www.thencbla.org and READ.gov.

The Exquisite Corpse Adventure educational materials, available on the NCBLA's website at www.thencbla.org, could not have been created without expert help from the Butler Children's Literature Center (www.dom.edu/butler), particularly Thom Barthelmess, Marilyn Ludolph, Susan Roman, and the gifted faculty and graduate students from Dominican University's

Graduate Schools of Education and Library Science. Susannah Harris, Tina Chovanec, and Rachael Walker created wonderful interactive young people's projects for PBS/WETA's Reading Rockets (www.readingrockets.org) and AdLit.org (www.adlit.org).

Tens of thousands of our nation's young people, as well as young people around the world, have become fans of *The Exquisite Corpse Adventure*. We thank them for sharing their interest and enthusiasm with us and hope they continue their own remarkable reading and writing adventures!

Mary Brigid Barrett
The National Children's Book
and Literacy Alliance

John Y. Cole
The Center for the Book
in the Library of Congress